PRIZE

A SCI-FI ALIEN WARRIOR ROMANCE

BARBARIANS OF THE SAND PLANET
BOOK EIGHT

TANA STONE

BROADMOOR BOOKS

CHAPTER ONE

Cat stormed down the corridor, not bothering to nod politely at the passengers walking by. Luckily, they were busy chatting about what they planned to do once the pleasure cruiser reached Darnithian Prime and didn't even notice her flaming face and fisted hands. Not that she cared.

She knew her temper got her in trouble, but at that moment, she didn't care that she was channeling every Italian ancestor she'd ever had. Cat hoped the dark curses she was muttering in Italian would work on the passenger who'd just called her an idiot. It would be nice to see the woman covered in boils.

"I am so over this." She barely paused for the door to the steward's storage room to slide open before barreling inside and pacing a tight circle between the shelves inset in the steel walls. "Cassidy Bowen can bite me."

"Now that's something I wouldn't mind seeing."

Cat spun around, startled to see one of her fellow stewards sitting on a white, polymer crate. Her navy-blue uniform shirt was untucked, and her shoes had been kicked off. "Maya! What are you doing here?"

The woman with brown skin and black hair that spilled down her back in waves held up a thin, shiny flask. "The same thing you're doing, Catarina. Escaping from our high-maintenance passengers."

Cat eyed the flask. "I'm assuming you have something in there stronger than the watered-down drinks they're serving on the Nebula deck?"

She passed the flask to Cat with a wink. "Count on it. Dealing with people wealthy enough to travel in premier class across the galaxy requires some high-octane Cressidian gin."

Cat didn't hesitate before taking a swig of the alien drink, the liquor burning her throat as she swallowed. "I don't know how I got assigned to this deck, but it's going to take a lot more gin for me to make it through the voyage."

Maya took the flask back and took her own gulp. "What are you talking about? I heard you had the most customer service experience of anyone who applied."

Cat darted a glance to her friend. "Where did you hear that?"

Maya shrugged. "I hear things. I stand at a lot of cracked doors."

Cat tried to give her a stern look but ended up grinning. "You're saying you eavesdrop?"

"That makes it sound so tawdry. I merely keep my ears open. It's important to know what's going on, especially if you plan to work for the cruise liner for a while."

Cat sat down on the crate opposite her. "I guess so, but I don't plan to do this more than once."

"Really? Why not? The pay is decent. You get to travel through space." Maya waved a hand in the air. "The scenery is amazing."

Cat snorted out a laugh. "We see *so* much scenery as we run around waiting on the passengers."

Maya smiled. "Are you going to tell me what Cassidy Bowen did, that made you storm in here like you wanted to rip her head off?"

Cat huffed out a breath, much of her anger already dissipated by the booze and getting distance from the offending passenger. "She complained that I don't fold her towels into cool shapes. Apparently, Fran makes towel swans for all her passengers."

Maya made a face. "Fran is a suck-up."

"A suck-up who can make towel swans."

"This is a space cruise. Why is she spending time worrying about the towels in her room? She should be on the viewing deck, or watching a holographic movie, or at the spa. I hear the Neribbian masseuses are amazing."

"Well, they do have four hands."

She wagged a finger at Cat before passing her the flask. "That is an advantage."

Cat took another long drag and savored the burn of the alien booze as it seared her mouth and warmed her stomach. The potency of the alien gin uncoiled her tense shoulders and loosened her tongue. "The truth is, I shouldn't be here."

"Just because you can't make towel swans—?"

Cat shook her head, already a little lightheaded. "Because I lied to get the job."

Maya clamped her mouth closed. "So, you don't have the most hospitality experience?"

Cat choked back another laugh. "Not exactly."

"How much—?"

"None," Cat said quickly, then dropped her gaze to the floor. "I've never worked in hospitality or in customer service. To be honest, I'm not the kind of girl who should even be working on a cruise liner. I've got no family connections, no education, and no money."

Maya studied her for a moment. "Then I'm even more impressed that you managed to land a spot on this cruise liner. You must be a talented liar."

Cat's cheeks burned as she met her eyes. "I was desperate. There was nothing left for me on Earth, but without school or references, you can't even score an interview to clean toilets on this ship."

Maya's expression was sympathetic. "Why did you want to get on here so badly if you don't want to make a career of being a steward?"

Cat dragged a hand through her shoulder-length brown hair. "This cruise liner might be packed with rich bitches, but it means steady pay, which is something I've never had." She blew out a breath. "I guess I was tired of wondering where my next meal would come from, or how I'd make rent. There's no way to get ahead of you don't know somebody, and, officially, I know nobody."

"But now you're having second thoughts?"

Cat twitched one shoulder. "I didn't think the job would involve so much ass kissing. I'm not great at taking crap and kissing ass, a fact to which Cassidy Bowen would eagerly attest."

Maya laughed. "That blonde bitch wouldn't be happy with anything."

"You know her?"

"I've seen her around. She's the one who has ass implants and name drops so much it's like listening to her read a Forbes list, right?"

"A self-made billionaire, who just so happens to have borrowed her daddy's factories to make her designer lip gloss kits." Cat used air quotes on the words 'self-made' and 'billionaire.'

Maya rolled her eyes hard. "If they tipped well, it would be one thing, but this deck is notorious for tipping like crap. That's why they pay us more."

"Figures." Cat leaned back and rested her head against the shelves. "As depressing as my life was on Earth, at least I didn't have a spoiled brat bossing me around."

"Come on. You shouldn't give up so soon. We haven't even reached Darnithian Prime. Maybe you'll get lucky, and Cassidy will catch an alien virus and have to stay on the planet."

Cat crossed her fingers. "Let it be a virus that makes all her hair fall out."

"Or one that makes her skin turn green. Blondes do not look good with green skin." Maya leaned over and patted her knee. "Even if she doesn't come down with something that makes her sprout tentacles, there are always other cruises. Not every passenger will be as bad as her."

"If she doesn't get me fired before I can make it to another cruise."

"Don't worry," Maya said. "I'll put in a good word for you. I'll also tell Dev the bartender to slip some laxative into Cassidy's next cocktail."

Cat's throat tightened as she smiled. "Thanks. I know we haven't known each other long, but—"

Maya flapped a hand at her dismissively. "You're not the only one who started out with nothing. Grunge kids stick together, right?"

Normally, Cat would have flinched at the Earth slang for kids who came from the working class of the ravaged planet, but she liked the way Maya made it sound less like an insult and more like a badge of honor. "On one condition."

The woman cocked an eyebrow. "Which is?"

"You teach me how to make towel swans."

Maya tipped her head back and laughed. "I'll do you one better. I'll teach you how to make something fitting for Cassidy—a towel Kracken."

"You're so bad," Cat said, shaking her head.

"What are they going to do?" Maya asked. "Fire you mid-cruise? Kick you off while we're flying through space?"

Cat shuddered. "I hope not. Space freaks me out."

Maya took another swig of gin. "Anyone who lies to get a job waiting on the richest people on Earth—but in space, even though she's terrified of it—really wants it. You deserve to be here."

Before Cat could tell her that she did really want it, the ship shuddered and lurched to one side. Both women slid off the glossy crates and fell onto the floor. Another jolt sent them sliding in the other direction.

"What the hell?" Maya cried as the shelving units rattled, but their contents remained strapped in place.

The women attempted to help each other up as the ship continued to shake violently. When the sirens began wailing and red lights blared overhead, they exchanged a terrified look. When the order was given over the comms system to report to the escape pods and abandon ship, their eyes met, and they spoke in unison.

"Fuck."

CHAPTER TWO

Dev glanced at his younger Dothvek twin after they'd watched the bounty hunter ship take off from the planet's surface, sand flying around them and biting the skin of their bare chests. They were both disappointed that their attempt to join the human/Dothvek crew had been rebuffed, but Trek's scowl was deep, and his mood dark.

Trek cut his gaze to him, aware without Dev speaking that he was being inspected. Their species was known for being able to sense each other's emotions and sometimes thoughts, but his mental bond with his twin was much stronger. If they wished to be silent, they could communicate entirely without words, but they'd learned long ago that it made others nervous.

Still, it took no effort for Dev to sense his twin's disappointment. It was sadness he shared.

Having their Dothvek kinsmen visit had been wonderful, but it only served as a stark reminder that those warriors had found their mates and were starting families. Their lives were among the stars with the beautiful females, not on the sand planet with few females and little adventure, like Dev and Trek who remained in the Dothvek oasis village.

Dev pivoted to face the village. The high-peaked tents were clustered around a broad pond that was ringed by clusters of tall trees with tufted tops. Pens of furry jebels brayed and shuffled their wide, flat feet, while savory meat roasted over a spit, and filled the air with the smells of crackling skin and dripping fat. Tiny bells jingled on the flaps of the tents when the breeze passed through, and when it didn't, heat rose from the shimmering gold sand and warmed the furs in the tents.

The village had always been their home, as had the wide sands where they hunted and explored. They were made to live on the sands, their skin the same gold hue as the iridescent dunes, and the thick ridges sweeping out from their spines protecting them from the powerful rays of two suns. Dev and Trek had never even considered living anywhere else, until their kinsmen had found off-world mates and left the Dothvek home world for adventures as bounty hunters.

Although they were glad to stay behind and protect their people and defend the new ruler of their clan, Dev felt his brother's hunger for adventure as if it was his own. Now that they'd heard the stories of their kinsmen's adventures in space, the oasis village seemed small, and their prospects slim. The ache of longing to see other worlds welled up in his chest, and the desire to find mates was not going to fade quickly from either of their minds.

"We should consider Kyrana's suggestion," Trek said, once the gray hull was far enough above them that it vanished into the upper atmosphere.

Dev wrinkled his nose, startled by his brother's suggestion. "Crestek mates?"

"They're compatible, and many are desirable."

Dev scowled. He knew they'd forged a treaty with their former enemies, but it was hard to wipe away a lifetime of suspicion in a single agreement. The Cresteks and their desire for progress were the reasons that his planet had so few females, and that the two branches of the same family tree had been divided for so long. The creatures in the stone city had rejected the old ways, and the wisdom of the goddesses. They'd lost their ability to communicate with their minds, and their skills as powerful hunters and warriors. Instead of living in tents on the sands as their ancestors had done for millennia, the Cresteks had barricaded themselves behind walls, and lived in luxury.

Even though they had agreed to a truce and the two clans were coming together to trade, the idea of living in the Crestek city was unthinkable, and he suspected a pampered Crestek female would find the oasis village to be primitive. But the mated warriors aboard the bounty hunting vessel had made it very clear that he and his brother couldn't join their crew without mates. "What we need are females like the bounty hunters."

Trek jerked his head up impatiently and made a sharp click in his throat, his dark braid swinging. "There are no more female bounty hunters in the entire galaxy, and remember, we need two mates."

"We would be lucky to find one," Dev said under his breath, giving a final, longing glance at the empty space the ship had occupied.

"One?" Trek scoffed.

Dev glanced at his twin brother but didn't say what they both knew. He didn't need to. Twins were rare among their kind, which meant they shared an even stronger empathic bond. It also meant that they could share their bond with a single female. Because it had been generations since there had been twin Dothveks, the tales of the last pair of warriors mated to one female seemed fantastical. The mated trio was only occasionally whispered about anymore, and neither twin knew if they believed such a thing, or it was truly a myth.

Had a Dothvek female truly been mated to twin warriors? Had they shared a single tent and slept in the same furs? Had their children been shared between the three as one family? If it had ever truly happened, there was nothing left but the myth. No Dothveks today believed it as fact or possibility. Dothveks bonded with one female—their mind mate—that was fated and absolute. How could Dev and Trek share a mind mate, especially one who wasn't of their own species?

Myth or not, Dev and Trek had shared everything since they were boys, including their innermost thoughts. They fought in sync, moved in tandem, and communicated so seamlessly that even their Dothvek kinsmen had a hard time understanding their intuitive language. Would it be much different to share a female?

Dev looked up, realizing that his twin was easily reading his thoughts, his own brow furrowed. Trek was the younger of the two, and the more impetuous and excitable, but even he was hesitant and doubtful about such a thing. Before they could talk about it, something rumbled high above them.

Peering up into the almost-white sky, Dev saw nothing until a spiral of smoke appeared, almost like a wisp. Then the spiral continued to curl down and arch into the distance, leaving a trail of smoke behind it. They couldn't see where it finally disappeared, but it had landed somewhere in the middle of the sands.

Trek grasped his brother's arm. Without exchanging a word, they knew exactly what the other was thinking. The bounty hunter females had arrived on the planet in a burst of flame and smoke, crashing somewhere on the sands, where K'alvek had found them. Could they be so lucky?

Dev stilled himself, sending his mind out as far as it could reach and forcing himself to ignore his brother's swirl of impulsive thoughts. There was a new consciousness on the sands. He sensed her fear and anger. *Her.*

The Dothvek warrior's heart stuttered in his chest. The creature he sensed was a female. He was sure of it. He didn't know what species she was, but she clearly wasn't Dothvek or Crestek, if she'd come from off-world.

Exhaling and focusing his empathic abilities on her, Dev picked up a flurry of frustration and confusion. She hadn't landed on their planet on purpose. She'd crashed.

He gripped his brother's arm as panic swept through him then faded. She wasn't hurt. At least, she wasn't in pain. But she was very irate. He could almost hear the curses echoing across the sands. Then he was almost felled by a strange sensation that slammed into him like a towering wave.

Dev swiveled his head to meet his brother's gaze, the same expression of shock on Trek's face that he felt. Had they both sensed the same pull, the undeniable draw, to the female?

"We must find her," Dev said.

Trek nodded, his eyes blazing. It was too much to wonder out loud if she could possibly be one of their future mates. Or both.

Then twin warriors took off running across the dunes, their hearts pounding and their legs pumping. They would soon find out.

CHAPTER
THREE

Cat stumbled from the pod and fell onto the sand, cursing as she face-planted, and got a mouthful of the powdery substance that glittered in the bright sunlight. She spluttered as she spit and wiped at her mouth, only succeeding in smearing more sand across her face.

"What the hell?" She managed to stand, even though her feet sank up to her calves, and she put a hand up to shield her eyes as she scanned her surroundings, which consisted of rolling dunes as far as she could see, and two suns overhead. "Where the holy hell am I?"

She turned back to the escape pod she'd arrived in, noting that it was wedged into the sand with only the nose buried. Wrenching her feet from the sand, she managed to get back to the pod and stick her head inside. She wasn't a specialist in space vessels—or any type of machine—but she remembered enough from her training to know that she should attempt to send a transmission. Her emergency beacon should be automatically activated, but she needed to let the command crew of the cruiser know where she was.

Cat cut another glance at the desert surrounding her. Wherever the hell she was.

As she fiddled with the controls, she cursed Cassidy Bowen again. "If only I hadn't been so busy getting that prima donna to her escape shuttle, I might not have been stuck taking one of the last pods off the cruiser."

Swiping the back of her hand across her gritty brow, she huffed out a hot breath as sweat rolled down her face. At least Maya had been with her when she'd deployed. Her friend and fellow steward had been by her side as they'd done their jobs and steered all the passengers from their deck to the luxury emergency shuttles. Despite Cassidy's loud protests that the sirens were giving her a migraine and interrupting her afternoon nap, she'd finally been loaded into the plush vessel that was captained by one of the crew.

"She's probably on some alien world being wined and dined already."

Although they hadn't gotten a lot of information before being told to get their passengers to the escape shuttles, the word passed furtively from steward to steward as they'd calmly shepherded people down the corridors was that the ship had encountered an unexpected meteor field. Despite the ship's defenses, one of the larger objects took out an engine and caused hull breaches followed by fires inside the cruiser. Getting the passengers off was a precaution, but it would also allow the ship to be repaired before resuming flight.

The shuttles would be flown to a nearby Class-M planet, where the passengers would be given accommodations while the ship underwent repairs. The stewards would join the passengers and resume their roles tending to them until they were returned to their ship.

"Because of course we would," Cat muttered under her breath. "Heaven forbid the elite class passengers lift a finger."

But, unless she was mistaken, Cat hadn't ended up on the Class-M planet with the rest of the crew. There were no other escape pods or shuttles in sight, and she doubted the cruise liner captain would purposefully choose a desert planet with seemingly no life. She didn't spot a single outpost or building, much less a town or city where an entire ship's complement could stay.

"This is because I was one of the last ones off." Cat squinted at the controls and the navigational coordinates she'd inputted before taking off. She'd been so preoccupied by having to cajole Cassidy that she'd barely paid attention when Maya had told her the coordinates of the destination planet. Then when she'd finally gotten into the pod, she'd remembered the numbers but not the order.

"Fricking dyslexia." She read the coordinates she'd entered, sure now that she'd flipped around enough of the numbers that she'd ended up far from everyone else.

Her eyes burned with frustrated tears as the numbers blurred. "Serves you right for lying to get on the ship. You never should have been on the cruiser in the first place, and you had no business being a steward."

Cat's one small consolation was that she had successfully loaded every passenger under her charge into their shuttle. At least she could feel good about that. She might not have been qualified for her job, but she'd done it. The elite passengers were safe and sound—and she was...

She found the comms buttons and pressed the one that would allow her to send out a transmission, but nothing happened when she pushed it. Cat poked it again and then once more, but it was dead. She swiveled her head around the cockpit, which was void of any blinking lights or the humming of the engine. Was the entire thing dead in the water? Or, in this case, the sand?

For the first time in her life, Cat wished she'd paid more attention in her science classes, or even in the orientation for the cruise liner. They'd gotten a thorough run-down of the escape pods, but she'd been so nervous about getting the job and worried that someone would see through her ploy, that she hadn't paid as much attention as she should have.

"Story of my fucking life." She flopped back in the pod's seat, grateful that it was slightly cooler sheltered from the desert heat. Then she gave herself a mental shake and sat up. "It's okay. This is only a minor setback. Once the ship's crew picks up my pod's emergency beacon, they'll come for me."

She tried not to think about how far down on the list of priorities one errant escape pod was for a crew dealing with a damaged ship and relocated passengers. At the very least, she could count on Maya to notice her missing and send up an alarm.

"Until then, I guess I'm stuck on this ball of sand."

It wasn't so bad, she thought, as she reclined in the comfortable pod seat. The escape pod wasn't huge, but it shielded her from the blazing suns. She reached up and opened one of the inset cabinets, retrieving a metal cylinder of water and a couple of shiny ration pouches. Not to mention, it was well equipped for survival. *That* she did remember from orientation. She could hang in the pod comfortably until her rescue arrived.

Feeling better about her situation, Cat took a swig of cool water. She hadn't even swallowed when the pod shifted abruptly and started to sink into the sand.

So much for that.

CHAPTER
FOUR

Trek pumped his legs easily as they raced over the dunes, skidding down the steep hills of sand and kicking up shimmering clouds behind him. His older brother—by only a few heartbeats—ran by his side, and there was no talking between them—only the sounds of their breath.

They didn't need to talk. He'd always preferred communicating through their minds, even when it had bothered others that they took so long to speak as children. The best things were passed between their minds, and no mere words could convey the excitement and trepidation he was experiencing as they barreled toward something completely unknown but filled with possibility.

Trek straightened one leg in front of him and used it to glide down a particularly high peak of sand, grunting when he reached the bottom and a puff of sand rose around him. The heat of the sun beat down of his bare back, but he welcomed the warmth. There was nowhere he'd rather be than on the sands with his twin brother, and his chest swelled as they rushed forward in tandem.

Dev raised an arm high, his finger pointing to the streak still visible across the nearly white sky. It was fading, but that didn't mean they couldn't track it. Sand serpents weren't the only things the brothers could track over the dunes, and Trek's instincts told him to pivot slightly as they drew closer to the impact site.

Although the bounty hunter ship had crashed onto the Dothvek planet, it had been their kinsman K'alvek who'd found it. Since then, ships had come and gone with more regularity, but streaks across the sky were not something they saw often. And Trek had never been struck by such a strong sense that the creature in the vessel needed him.

He glanced at his brother. Needed them.

Dev had shared the same feelings. Trek had felt them pulsing through him just as strongly, even though they hadn't spoken of it. They didn't need to.

At the top of the next dune, Dev threw an arm across Trek's chest to stop him. They heaved in hot breaths as they surveyed the scene below. There was no massive ship hunched on the sand and dwarfing the surrounding dunes. There was only a small, shiny cylinder that was white on the outside, and had rounded ends. A mass of fabric that matched the vessel was attached by a series of strings, and it struck Trek that the fabric had been used to slow the descent.

Trek had always been fascinated by how things worked, even though his people did not embrace technology. He'd snuck onto the bounty hunter ship when his kinsmen had visited and explored the engine room, steering clear of the fiery-haired engineer who was protective of her engines. Now, almost as much as he longed to learn who was inside the vessel, he wanted to see how it worked.

"She is there," Dev said, his voice a gravelly rumble. "Somewhere."

Trek nodded. He felt it, too. He felt her.

Without another word, the twin warriors slid down the dune. When they hit the bottom, the vessel shifted suddenly, tipping forward and sinking into the sand.

Trek's stomach lurched along with the sand as he sensed a burst of panic that wasn't his own. She was inside the sinking vessel.

He and Dev darted forward, reaching the open hatch of the odd little ship as powdery sand poured into it. A female with dark hair sat inside, struggling to stand. She coughed and waved a hand in front of her face as sand filled the air.

It wasn't how he'd envisioned meeting the creature he and Dev had sensed from across the sands, but they didn't have time to introduce themselves. They had to get her out before the sand swallowed her and her ship.

He grabbed one of her hands and Dev grabbed the other, and they yanked her from the ship. She was jerked free, and they all stumbled back. He and Dev landed on their backs and the female ended up sprawled on top of them. Behind them, the vessel was devoured by the desert, disappearing entirely as the sand sucked it down and then was placid and smooth once again.

"My pod!" The female scrambled up from them, spinning around and throwing her arms into the air. "It's gone. Now how the hell am I supposed to get off this ball of sand?"

Trek exchanged a glance with his brother. This female reminded him more of Tori—a Zevrian female with a bad temper who was their kinsman Vrax's mate—than of one of the sweet, smiling humans they'd met. He stood, as did Dev, and brushed the sand off his bare skin and animal skin pants as he watched her fume and mutter to herself.

When she spun around again, she seemed to notice them for the first time, yelping and slapping a hand over her mouth. "You're not...."

Whatever she'd thought they were died on her lips as she looked them up and down, her eyes widening. It wasn't lost on Trek that the Dothveks were very different from humans. He'd grown accustomed to the strange, small creatures who had no ridges, but he was aware that this creature had probably never seen a Dothvek before.

She eyed them suspiciously before cutting her gaze to the spot where her ship had vanished. "I guess I should thank you for saving me from getting sucked down into the sand."

Trek gave her a small bow, as did Dev.

Now that she faced him, he was able to look her up and down, as well. She was definitely human and certainly female, with dark hair that curled down her back, and curves beneath her form-fitting shirt that made his mouth go dry. Her eyes were also dark and her pink lips plump. Although her skin wasn't the rich shade of gold theirs was, it was tan. Still, he doubted she would survive long under their suns without feeling the effects.

She waved one arm over her head. "Where is this?" She yelled the words and said them so slowly trek wondered if the suns were already affecting her.

"You are on the sands," Dev said. "Not far from the Dothvek village."

She jerked up. "You can understand me?"

Trek tapped his ear and the universal translator that the bounty hunter females had given everyone in their clan. "We can understand you, human."

She sighed. "Good. My name is Cat, and I need to find the cruise liner I was on before I had to abandon ship."

"I am Dev, and this is my twin brother Trek. We can take

you to safety off the sands, but we do not know how to find your ship. For now, you must stay on our planet."

CHAPTER
FIVE

Cat met the alien's serious gaze. Did he just say she'd have to stay? Well, that wasn't going to work.

"Stay?" She swung her head to take in the vast expanse of sand that stretched around her for as far as she could see. "Here? There's nothing but sand. I can't stay here."

"There is much more than sand," the other alien said with a frown. "And there are many things under the sand that are unseen."

She dropped her gaze to the shimmering gold sand that was so powdery the slightest breeze lifted it up and swirled it into the air. Under the sand? Pulling her feet from the sand, she shuddered at what that might mean.

This had all been a huge mistake—lying to get the job on the star cruiser, going into space, crashing onto a sand planet. She wasn't cut out for space travel, and she definitely wasn't cut out for living in a desert—even if the natives were jaw-dropping.

Cat was trying her hardest not to stare, but they had to be almost seven feet tall and solid muscle. Even though they were bipedal and humanoid, any chance of them being mistaken for humans had vanished with their gold skin and the ridges on their back, not to mention their pointed ears. They wore their dark hair flowing down their backs, the inky blackness matching the tattoos ringing their forearms. She let her gaze drop to their corded stomach muscles. Sweet Mary and Joseph, were those more ridges running beneath the low-hanging waistbands of their pants?

"Like my brother said, there is more to our planet than sand."

She jerked her gaze back to their faces, nodding absently. At first glance, she'd assumed the hulking males were barbarians, but they could communicate, and they clearly had some access to technology if they had universal translators, although they weren't permanent implants, which made her think that the innovation had only recently reached them.

"I'll have to take your word for it." She peered up at the scorching suns and wiped a hand across her slick forehead. "You said something about a village nearby? I'm assuming you have water there?"

The aliens had said they were twins, and she could see their similarities, but she also noticed the small ways in which they set themselves apart. One had a braid woven down the side of his long hair, while the other's fell loose, the ends lightening to a paler brown.

"You wish to go back to our village?" the alien with the braid said, the eagerness brimming in his voice.

"That's probably the best place to wait for a rescue, right?"

The aliens exchanged a glance before the other brother tilted his head at her. "It is, although not many ships grace our planet. Our peoples have not welcomed trade or contact with off-worlders until recently."

"So, there's no shipyard where I can catch a transport?"

More confused looks and head shaking. "Shipyard?"

"You know, a place where spaceships land and refuel before loading up and taking off again." Maybe she'd been wrong to so quickly dismiss the idea that this was a barbarian planet.

"There is no such thing here," one of the brothers said while the other lifted his chin and made a clicking sound with his tongue. "Not even the Cresteks have such a place."

Cat didn't know who the Cresteks were, but from the way both brothers curled their lips, she guessed they weren't well-respected. Even so, she would have made friends with a Dragonian pirate if it meant finding her crew and her friend Maya. She wouldn't even mind seeing Cassidy Bowen about now.

She groaned and rubbed her sweaty temple. "The heat is clearly getting to me if I'm thinking Cassidy isn't so bad."

"Cassidy?" One of the aliens said. "Is that your name?"

"My name?" She choked back a laugh. "Nooooooo. My name is Catarina, but my friends call me Cat."

"Catarina," the alien with the braid said. "That is a beautiful name, but I would like to call you what your friends call you."

"I would like to call you Cat, as well," the other brother added quickly. "Would you consider me one of your friends?"

Her mouth twitched as how eagerly the aliens were tripping over each other to call her by her nickname. "That's fine. I guess since you both did save me from sinking into the sand, we're officially friends."

"Friends," the other brother said with a smile, but the way he said the word sent a tingle down her spine.

"Not that this will be much of a long friendship," she said. "I really can't stay her for any longer than it takes to get a rescue shuttle to take me back to the rest of my crew."

The two aliens glanced at each other before nodding, and

she got the strangest feeling that they were communicating without talking, not that such a thing was possible, was it?

"Remind me again of your names," Cat said, embarrassed that she'd forgotten them so quickly, but chalking it up to the blazing heat and the shock of crashing on the planet and being snatched from a sinking escape pod.

"Trek," the brother with the braid said, jerking a thumb toward his counterpart. "Dev."

She committed that to memory. "And you're twins?"

"I am older," Dev said, gaining him a dark look from Trek.

"By only a handful of heartbeats," Trek muttered under his breath.

Cat couldn't help grinning at the two aliens. Despite living on a planet on the other side of the galaxy, they had much in common with human males. Although, truth be told, they were about a thousand times hotter and buffer than any human man she'd ever seen in real life. As she was allowing her mind to wander and her gaze to return to their bare skin and the dark tattoos emblazoned on it, she felt a faint rumble beneath her feet.

Dev and Trek spun and assumed a battle stance, flipping curved blades from their waistbands with lightning speed. But it wasn't an attacking army that emerged over the sand dune —it was a stampede of long-legged, furry animals with wide feet that seemed to fly across the sand.

"Jebels!" Trek glanced at his brother. "Why are they running?"

Dev's brow creased as he leveled a finger at the sky and the dark swarm quickly approaching. "They're running from that."

CHAPTER SIX

Dev sensed the fear in the jebels as they thundered toward them, the sand kicking up behind their wide, flat feet and creating a shimmering gold cloud that rose to meet the darker cloud descending.

"What the hell is that?" Cat asked, her shaky voice barely carrying above the din of hooves and the buzzing of the insect swarm.

"*Hashara*," Trek answered, before his brother could. "Insects that descend onto the sands once every rotation around the suns."

"Insects?" Cat wrapped her arms around herself and shuddered. "What kind of insects?"

"They won't harm you," Trek said, "but they do eat everything in sight, and make a lot of noise."

Dev frowned as the jebels got closer, reaching out his mind to calm them. But the animals, normally so receptive to him, would not be calmed. They knew all too well the feel of the winged insects on their fur and the deafening sound of chirping that would engulf them.

"I don't care if they won't harm me." Cat began to back away. "I hate flying insects, and if they're anything like cockroaches, I'm going to lose my mind."

Dev didn't know what a cockroach was or if the human was being truthful that she would misplace her brain, but he also knew they couldn't stay and allow themselves to be overtaken by the swarm.

He cut a quick look to his brother and jerked his head toward the jebels. *We can catch a ride.*

We'll never make it to the village in time, Trek replied.

His younger brother was right. The swarm was moving fast, and even the jebels couldn't outrun it for that long. Then something occurred to him. *Rukken!*

Trek wrinkled his forehead in confusion. *He's on the bounty hunter ship far from our planet. I doubt he can help us now, brother.*

His camp. The tent he used when he was an exile. Dev waved a hand behind them. *It isn't far from here. We can make it there.*

"Um, guys?" Cat stumbled in the soft sand as she backed up more. "It's getting closer."

Trek gave his older brother a curt nod before scooping the female up by the waist and running toward the stampeding jebels.

Dev growled in frustration that his brother had beaten him to the female, but he pushed that aside as he focused on the animals barreling down and ran toward them. When he'd almost reached the herd, he pivoted quickly and started to run with the beasts, matching his pace with theirs. He saw that Trek was doing the same, even as the human yelped and struggled in his grasp.

The dunes shook from the pounding hooves as the sand was churned, but Dev wasn't frightened by the size of the jebels or their speed. He ran neck and neck with a jebel, resting a hand on its furry mane and sending it calming energy before threading his fingers into the matted fur and swinging himself onto the animal's back.

For a moment, the creature was startled. After all, this wasn't one of the jebels they'd domesticated and kept in a pen at the village. This was a wild jebel who ran free on the sands and wasn't accustomed to riders on its back. Dev concentrated his thoughts on calming the creature, patting the brown fur as they continued to race across the desert and from the impending swarm.

Swiveling his head to one side, Dev spotted Trek and the female still running between the jebels. His younger brother had never been as good with animals. Although he was a skilled rider, he preferred objects to creatures and had never mastered the art of using his thoughts to train jebels like Dev.

After a small burst of satisfaction that he was astride a jebel and his brother was not, he conceded that getting the female onto a beast as well as himself was not an easy feat. He doubted the human had ever ridden a beast like a jebel, if she'd ridden any animal at all.

Dev fisted his hands in the jebels mane and used his hands as well as his thoughts to steer the creature toward his brother. Once he was behind Trek, he kicked at the jebel's flank with his heels, urging the creature forward so he could lean down and grab the female by the back of her pants. He snatched her from Trek and plopped her down in front of him.

Trek twisted his head, scowled, and then accepted Dev's outstretched arm and heaved himself onto the jebel behind his brother. Dev wrapped his arms around the female and gripped the jebel's mane, leaning forward and cocooning her smaller body as he directed the beast from the herd and toward the old camp site of their formerly exiled kinsman.

The buzzing of the insects had grown louder, and Dev chanced a peek over his shoulder. Instead of a dark mass, he could now see the individual flying creatures, with their wildly beating, diaphanous wings. He exchanged a solemn look with his brother and turned back around, kicking the sides of the jebel, and making a clicking sound in the back of his throat to spur on the animal.

The rest of the herd peeled off in one direction, but Dev remembered the location of Rukken's old campsite from the position of the suns, and he kept the jebel heading toward it. As far as he knew, Rukken had left his old home standing, even though he now lived on a spaceship. When he'd been asked why he kept the tent out on the sands, he'd said it held good memories, and was a good place to escape to with his mate. Dev hoped it would be a good place to escape from a *hashara* swarm.

Cresting a tall dune, he almost cheered when he spotted the small tent huddled beside a pond and copse of trees and bushes. Glancing behind him once more and seeing that the swarm had not followed the rest of the herd, he gritted his teeth and urged the jebel forward.

Dev sensed his brother's elation at finding the tent and also a pulse of relief from Cat. He tightened his grip around her, her feelings sending a possessive thrill through him.

He could sense her. It hadn't been a fluke, and he hadn't imagined it. Her emotions were swirling within him more subtly than his brother's, but they were there.

His excitement was tempered by the roar of the swarm that was now so close he could feel the air shifting from the beating wings. Racing down the dune, the jebel slipped but righted itself, running at full speed toward the tent.

The moment they reached it, Dev slid off the creature's back, pulling Cat with him. Trek leaped down from the jebel and rushed forward, pushing the tent flaps aside and jerking the female inside with him. Without pausing to think, Dev followed them with the jebel, crowding into the tent and tying the flaps closed behind him just as thousands of *hashara* pelted the sides and swallowed the tent in their buzzing.

"Really brother?" Trek asked, swatting away the jebel's tail as they all stood, panting.

Cat leaned forward and braced her hands on her knees. "Now what?"

"Now we wait until it's safe to leave," Dev said, thumping the jebel's sweaty flank.

"Here?" Cat swiveled her head around the compact interior that only had one pile of furs. "All of us?"

CHAPTER
SEVEN

Cat gaped at the inside of the tent. It hadn't looked like much from the outside, and interior was just as simple. A thick, wooden pole ran up in the middle, and buff-colored fabric swept out from the top. The floor was sand, but was covered by animal skins and rough-hewn fabric, with a pile of thicker furs and blankets forming a bed to one side.

"How long do we all have to be stuck in here?" She took a step back as the furry animal that looked like a humpless camel, but furrier, attempted to walk around the cramped space. She'd never seen an actual camel, of course. Those had gone extinct on Earth long ago, but she'd seen digital images.

Trek lifted his head as the insects continued to shake the tent fabric. "Until the swarm passes."

Cat stifled an impatient sigh. "How long does that usually take?"

The other brother, Dev, thumped the animal on its rump as it shuffled around inside the tent. "Appearances of the swarm aren't common, so I do not know for certain, but it should be safe to leave by the time the suns rise again."

Cat unwound his words. "Tomorrow? We have to stay crammed in here all night?"

The other brother shot Dev a look but shrugged. "We could leave sooner, but the suns will set, and the sands will darken, and it will be more dangerous."

"There is more dangerous stuff out there than swarms of flying bugs?"

"Much more dangerous," Dev said, his deep voice filling the tent with warning. "I would not risk you on the sands at night."

A black-winged creature flew through a gap in the tent flaps, buzzing as it circled the pole, and then swooped down at their heads. Cat shrieked and flapped her hands over her head. Why did it have to be flying bugs? Give her snakes, spiders, rabid dogs. None of them made her skin crawl like scuttling insects with wings.

Trek whipped a curved blade off his waistband and sliced it through the air, striking the insect and cutting it in half. The two parts of the creature fell to the ground, and Trek gave a satisfied grunt while hooking his blade back onto his waist. The furry animal bent down and nibbled on the dead bug while Dev tightened the ties on the tent and shot his brother a look.

Cat focused on breathing in and out—and avoiding watching the alien camel munch on the bug—as she processed the fact that the disgusting flying bugs were the least of her worries on the alien desert. She'd landed on an alien planet that appeared to be mostly desert and had clouds of insects that weren't even the scariest thing out there. Despite her deep breaths, panic fluttered in her chest like a bird trying to escape from a cage.

"This is insane. I can't be here. I'm supposed to be with the rest of the crew on a friendly planet. Actually, I'm supposed to be on a cruise liner making sure Cassidy Bowen's every need is met. I can't be on a random sand planet that doesn't even have a shipyard or regular flights in and out. This is all wrong."

Both twin aliens stared at her. She knew she sounded crazy, but she couldn't help it. Everything was going wrong. It had been going wrong for over a decade, but this was too much. She could handle scraping by with barely enough to eat, but now that she'd finally managed to sweet talk her way into a better world and get a chance to have a better life, it was slipping through her fingers like the sand that surrounded her.

Her heart raced faster as the tent seemed to grow smaller and hotter. It didn't help that the alien camel smelled funny, and she knew she was being unreasonable. The two huge aliens had saved her from being sucked under the sand and gotten her to safety when the swarm of insects had pursued them. She should be grateful. But somehow all she could muster was panic and fear.

She sucked in a warm breath, backing away until her head brushed the top of the tent. "If I don't find a way off this planet, the cruiser will leave without me, and I'll never have the chance to be discovered. Fuck, I won't even get paid."

"If you wish to leave, we will help you leave," Trek said.

His brother swung his gaze to him, holding it for a beat before nodding. "We will help you leave if that is what you wish, but if you attempt to leave now you will only be walking into the swarm."

That gave her pause. The idea of walking into a swarm of insects did not appeal. She pressed a hand to her chest, feeling her heart slow a bit. "You'll help me leave?"

Dev jerked his head up quickly and made a sharp clicking

noise with his tongue, but Trek moved his head up and down. "If that is what you wish."

"We cannot promise transport until our kinsmen return in their ship." Dev's gaze was trained on the furry neck of the animal as he stroked it.

"That's okay." Cat exhaled a long breath. "I'm sure my crew will pick up the escape pod's beacon, and they'll send a rescue."

The two alien warriors glanced at each other quickly, but she noticed the look that passed between them.

"You don't believe me?"

Dev cleared his throat, his hand pausing on the creature's neck. "We have never left our planet, or been in a ship among the stars, but not all ships find it easy to locate our world."

The nerves that had subsided started to flit again. "Do you have some kind of transmission-blocking satellites, or security force fields?"

Trek jerked his head up and made the same sharp click his brother had. "We have nothing like that, but our planet has its own mind when it comes to off-worlders. The goddess energy does not always welcome outsiders."

Cat stared at him, wondering if he was being serious about goddess energy and planets having minds of their own. "Well, the cruiser I was on is one of the most high-tech, luxury space liners flying today. It's got the most sophisticated equipment available, so if anyone can find me, they can."

Dev met her eyes, his own dark ones flashing with heat. "Then we will wait for your rescuers."

Her mouth went dry, and she pulled her gaze from his, taking another step back. "Okay, then. Worst-case scenario, I wait for your friends to return in their ship and hitch a ride with them. How long until they come back to the planet?"

The alien twins passed another inscrutable look between

them before Dev answered. "We do not know. Their visits are not set, but there are usually many cycles of the moon between them."

She shifted her gaze from one to the other. "Months? You mean they won't come back here for months? I could be stuck here for months?"

"Not if you are rescued first," Trek said with a grin.

"But for now, you should get some rest." Dev inclined his head to the furs.

Cat slid her gaze to the huge camel creature, and then to the huge gold-skinned, bare-chested aliens. She wasn't sure with which of them she was more nervous about sharing a tent.

CHAPTER
EIGHT

Trek released a breath as the human arranged herself on the furs with a few backward glances at them. She was human, like most of the bounty hunter females who'd come to their planet, but she was very different from them. For one, she didn't seem thrilled to be traveling through space, and even less excited to be on an unfamiliar world. She wasn't a trained fighter, or even someone who was used to life among the stars. Most importantly, she had no intention of staying any longer than absolutely required.

He and Dev had been honest with her about their planet. It had remained unexplored and uncolonized, while other worlds had become the home to outposts and refueling stations. The Dothveks believed the planet's energy force, or goddess energy was what had kept them safe from invaders and those who would exploit it. Not that many could look at their hot, sand planet and see anything worth exploiting.

They hadn't told her everything, though. Their world was not so isolated that word could not be sent to the bounty hunters. The Crestek city even maintained communications systems, and their new treaty provided the Dothveks with access to the technology. Trek scowled at this. As if he would allow Cat to get anywhere near the Cresteks with their materialistic means of luring females to them.

We can't keep her on the sands forever.

Trek cut his eyes to his brother as Dev patted the jebel's neck, acknowledging the statement with a grunt.

I have no intention of keeping her anywhere. He pointed to the fabric ceiling and the shadows of the insects striking the outside as the light from the suns faded. *Would you have us take her out in this?*

Dev gave him a look that told Trek he knew his mind as well as his own. *She is not like the other females.*

Trek pivoted and faced the tent flaps, bending to check that they were fastened tightly at the bottom. *Don't you think I know that? Don't you think I can sense her fear?*

Dev was silent for a beat, even the flurry of his thoughts stilling. *You can sense her thoughts?*

Trek craned his neck back, looking up at his brother and cocking one slash of a dark eyebrow. *You thought it was only you?*

Trek stood and could see from his brother's startled expression that he had believed he was the only one who'd picked up the female's thoughts and sensed the messy tangle of her emotions. He laughed as he thumped a hand on Dev's arm. *Our minds are as linked as any two can be. Did you not think we would not share this?*

Dev frowned. *We have not shared all things before.*

Trek thought of the females they'd each bedded before. No, they hadn't shared that, but those had been quick encounters with no mind connection. They'd both been eager recreational partners for the Dothvek priestesses in training who would take no mind mates but were free to enjoy males as they wished. The more Trek dwelled on it, the more he wondered if they'd perhaps shared those females as well without realizing it. There were only so many of the priestesses, and he'd enjoyed sampling almost all of them.

Dev cleared his throat, and Trek realized that he'd been remembering his encounters in vivid detail, which his brother could easily sense. He dropped his gaze to the ground but couldn't stop the grin twitching his lips.

There is no point in keeping her here and trying to see if she could be one of our mates if she is determined to leave.

Trek snapped his head up at his brother. *But I've already sensed her more powerfully than I have any other female before. Even when we pursued the shape-shifting bounty hunter, I didn't detect any special connection.*

Dev inclined his head as the jebel shifted his thick, padded hooves on the sand. *Neither did I, aside from the fact that she was beautiful and not taken.*

Her availability did not last long. Trek thought back to almost coming to blows with one of his Dothvek elders over the pretty female, and shame heated his cheeks. It had not been his finest moment—or Dev's. *But this female has no other suitors. No one knows about her presence on our planet.*

Dev jerked his head up and made a clicking noise in the back of his throat. *None of that matters if she doesn't wish to stay.*

We don't wish to stay.

Dev held his brother's gaze. She does not even wish to be in space. *Do you truly think this fragile creature would wish to join the bounty hunter crew with us?*

Trek jerked his head away. He hated when his older brother was right. Why did he have to sense a mind connection to someone who was so ill-suited to adventure, or even to the concept of space travel? He looked back at Dev. *There has to be a reason why I can sense her so strongly.*

Why we *can sense her so strongly.*

Trek rubbed a hand across his wrinkled brow. None of this made any sense, but the fact remained that they'd found a female stranded on the sands and saved her—twice. Now they were stuck in a tent with her until the danger passed. Maybe they had such a strong connection because of the dramatic circumstances. Maybe it was no more than a temporary link that would fade. Part of him wished that were true, and another part of him wished it wasn't.

It wasn't like she wasn't a desirable creature. She might not have gold skin or ridges, but he'd grown accustomed to females who didn't look Dothvek. He found her dark features and mane of dark curls to be intriguing and wouldn't mind tangling his fingers in her hair and holding it tight while he—

"Okay, which one of you said that?"

Trek jerked at Cat's words, as did his brother.

The female was sitting up and facing them, her wide eyes sliding from one to the other.

Dev cut a quick glance to him. "We said nothing."

"Not out loud, you didn't, but I heard what you said in my mind. Or I could feel it." She shook her head brusquely. "I don't know which, but all I know is that I didn't think those things."

Trek stopped breathing. He didn't need to look at his brother to know that Dev was in a state of shock. It was one thing for them to sense her. They were Dothveks and their species was known for their empathic abilities. She was human, known for being fragile and lacking in mental abilities like theirs. It was another thing entirely if this human female could pick up on their thoughts. A burst of elation filled him at what this could mean.

"Hey!" Cat jumped up and glared at both of them. "Who are you calling fragile?"

The good feeling evaporated, and his gut clenched. Good feeling gone.

CHAPTER NINE

Cat stared down the two aliens, her anger doing a good job of covering up the fact that she was freaking out.

She'd been trying to get to sleep, even though the sand underneath the animal skins and woven mats wasn't all that soft, and the insects were still occasionally pelting the outside of the tent and reminding her of their creepy presence. On top of all that, she was supposed to share the space with a smelly, camel-like creature who seemed as unnerved by the insect swarm as her and two huge aliens who shared a lot of knowing looks she couldn't quite decipher.

Still, she'd managed to find a decent position and had buried her nose far enough under the furs that she wasn't breathing in alien sand camel. Then the thoughts had started flitting though her mind. At first, she'd assumed it was her own nerves. After all, it had been a crazy day, between having to abandon ship to landing on a desert planet to being rescued by twin aliens. No one would blame her mind for being crowded with thoughts. But they weren't *her* thoughts.

When the first words drifted into her brain, she brushed them aside and tried to clear her mind and go to sleep. But the words kept coming, Words that weren't her own. Finally, she'd gotten a strong mental image of one of the aliens fisting his hand in her hair and holding her head back while he...

She'd jumped up, sure that wasn't her, and even more certain after she saw the guilty looks on the aliens' faces, that they were the ones projecting things into her mind. When she heard one of them call humans fragile, she snapped.

"Hey!" Cat had jumped up and glared at both of them. "Who are you calling fragile?"

The alien called Dev held up his hands with the palms facing her. Obviously, this was a universal sign of surrender. "I apologize for what you heard." He shot his brother a dark look that wasn't hard to decipher. "We should explain."

"Are you some kind of alien sorcerers?" She looked from one to the other, thinking they didn't look like what she'd imagine wizards to look like.

Trek snorted a half laugh and Dev glared at him again.

"We do not possess any magical powers," Dev said, "but some species might think that our Dothvek abilities are supernatural."

"O-kay." That was vague.

"All Dothveks are naturally empathic," he continued. "We can sense emotions. Mostly within each other, but also in other species and in animals. It makes us skilled hunters and trackers."

My breath returned to normal as I processed this. "You can read minds?"

Trek jerked his head up, which I'd come to realize was their way of saying no. "Not usually."

"My brother means that since we are twins, we share a stronger than normal mind bond. We can converse easily with our minds. We can also converse mentally with other Dothveks, but only the ones with which we share a close bond. With all other creatures and species, we typically sense their emotions or intent."

Cat shook her head. "But I heard words in my head that weren't my own, and then I saw a metal image that definitely wasn't mine."

Trek shifted from one foot to the other, his gaze lowering. "Apologies. That was my fault."

She stared at him for a moment, memories of how firmly he'd grabbed her hair seared in her brain. Her cheeks heated even though the alien hadn't laid a finger on her. It had been a long time since anyone had desired her like that, and it stirred something dormant in her core. The sensation wasn't unpleasant, but it was strange to feel someone else's desire as if it were your own.

"If this mind thing is only supposed to be between Dothveks, why do I hear your thoughts?"

"You shouldn't," Trek said. "If I'd had any idea that you could—"

"It is possible that the stress of the day and the danger we've experienced together created this unusual bond between us," Dev interrupted his brother. "But we will ensure that we keep our thoughts shielded from you."

"You can do that?"

Dev gave a single, curt nod. "As empaths, we know how to discipline our minds. Some are better at it than others, but we should be able to keep our thoughts from seeping into your mind."

Cat's shoulders relaxed before something occurred to her. "What about my thoughts? If I can sense yours, can you sense mine?"

Both aliens were silent for a moment before Dev resumed

stroking the beast next to him. "I will be honest with you, Catarina. I sensed your mind, but I purposefully did not delve into it or allow myself to open to it."

"Oh," she met his gaze, and her mouth went dry at the intensity of it. "Thank you, I guess."

"I also sensed your mind and did not explore it," Trek said.

Cat cocked her head at him. "You were too busy thinking of things you'd like to do to me, weren't you?"

The alien opened and closed his mouth a few times, struck dumb by her comeback. Cat almost laughed at how pained and remorseful the alien looked—and she almost felt bad for making him squirm. Almost.

She was still processing the fact that these two aliens could basically read minds and that there was some sort of connection that sent their thoughts into her mind. For someone who'd spent the better part of the last few years alone—and preferred it that way, thank you very much—it was a lot to take in.

"Listen." She held up her hands in much the way Dev had. "I've never met mind-reading aliens, so I'm going to pretend none of what happened actually happened. You didn't know I could hear what you were thinking so I'm not going to hold it against you, but I would love it if you guys could avoid muddling my brain. All I want is to get back to the star cruiser, so I can finish up my tour and get paid. As cool as it might be, I don't want to mind meld with anyone, or stay on this planet for any longer than I have to."

She ignored the hurt look that flickered across Dev's face. "I appreciate you saving me and helping me get off the planet but until I actually leave, let's keep our minds and thoughts to ourselves and everyone will be happier. I know I will."

When she finished her tirade, she sucked in a breath.

"Understood." Dev gave the beast a firm pat. "The swarm

seems to have moved on, so I will take the jebel outside to sleep. I might not be able to read minds, as you claim I can, but I know you do not wish to sleep with this creature in your bed."

Before Cat could respond or thank him, Dev had quickly untied the tent flaps and steered the animal outside, leaving her standing in the tent with Trek. Without the huge four-legged creature, the space seemed much larger, although Trek no longer met her eyes.

"You should rest," he said before turning and flopping onto the floor at the far side. "If we are to get you off the planet quickly, there is a long journey involved."

Cat didn't need to sense his thoughts to pick up the chill in his words.

Good going, she told herself. You've just pissed off the only creatures who were helping you.

CHAPTER
TEN

Dev strode outside, pulling the jebel behind him more forcefully than he'd intended. The creature shook his head to loosen his grip, the furry wattle shaking under his chin as he made a low guttural sound of displeasure.

"Sorry," Dev muttered, untangling his fingers from the matted fur, and slowing his walk toward the pond behind the tent. He of all Dothveks should know how temperamental jebels could be, and how little they liked to be pushed. He'd known the creatures to lock their knees on the sands and refuse to move if they were nudged too fast.

The two trudged to the edge of the water, and Dev paused as the animal lowered his head and drank. After a moment, he crouched low and scooped up a few handfuls of the cool water and sipped it. After racing across the sands and sucking in more sand than he would have wished, the liquid was refreshing.

Tipping his head back, Dev noted that the suns had fallen beyond the dunes, and the sky was an inky shade of blue. The swarm of *hashara* had moved on, although Dev noticed that the leaves of the nearby bushes and trees were partially eaten away.

It could have been worse, he thought. Dev knew very well all the creatures that roamed the sands—and roamed beneath them. The *hashara* were an annoyance, but they were not deadly. The air wasn't cold, but he shivered at the thought of encountering a sand serpent with Cat.

At least she was safe inside Rukken's old tent. Until she leaves, he reminded himself. Cat had made it very clear that she had no intention of staying. Not that he'd expected she would. Why would a female who'd traversed the skies in a cruiser find anything about his world intriguing? Her world was one of fast ships and technology, while he was at home on the sands and with the jebels.

"It wasn't meant to be," he whispered to the jebel, who ignored him as he continued to noisily slurp the water.

Then why had their minds so easily linked? He'd never experienced a connection with anyone other than his brother. And now it had happened with an off-worlder who had no intention of staying or even of staying in space.

Dev jerked his head up brusquely. It didn't matter. She would leave, and he would forget her, and he and Trek would go on with their lives. "It's better this way."

"What way?"

He spun around, his heart racing when he saw Cat standing outside the tent. He'd been so focused on his own thoughts, and conscious of not listening in on hers, that he hadn't even heard her step outside.

"I thought you were sleeping," he said, without answering her question. "Not that I was listening in—"

"Relax." She gave him a small smile as she walked closer to him, the dunes behind her silhouetted against the night sky like swelling waves. "I didn't come out here to yell at you again. I know you and Trek aren't listening. I can't sense either of you anymore."

Did she look sad when she said that? Dev torn his gaze from her and looked at the rippling surface of the pond. "Isn't that what you wanted?"

Cat stood by his side and looked across the water. "It's been such an insane day—check that, an insane trip—that I don't know what I want anymore."

He snuck a look at her. "Coming to this planet has caused you distress?"

"Well, I did have to abandon ship and crashed here in an escape pod, so it's not like I'm here on a weekend getaway." Then she shook her head. "I'm sorry I'm being so snarky. I guess it's my default setting when I'm scared, and lately I've been pretty scared."

His heart squeezed at this admission. "You don't have to be scared around us. Trek and I would never harm you or allow any harm to come to you." He turned to face her. "You do now know much about the Dothveks, but we are a species that is ruled by the wisdom of the goddesses. We revere females above all else and would never let anything hurt you—including ourselves."

"I did not know that about your people. That's cool. So, are your rulers women?"

"Our ruler now is a woman, and she is the best leader our clan has ever had."

"That sounds about right. Back on Earth, the countries with women in charge usually turned out better. Not that there were enough women in charge to fix everything."

Dev realized he'd known humans, but he knew little about their home world. Only that most of them had left it. "Do you miss your home planet?"

"Earth?" Cat laughed. "It's a bit of a wasteland. Everyone who could get off, did. If you have resources, you can live well, but the rest of us scrape by. That's why I lied my way into the job on the space cruiser. I might hate space travel, but it beats Earth."

"I am sad for your planet. I must not have the protection from the goddess energy that our world does."

"It probably doesn't." She swiveled her head to take in the sky, the tall frond-topped trees at the bank of the pond, and the undulating dunes surrounding them. "For a giant pile of sand, this place isn't so bad at night."

Dev bristled. "Our world is more than sand."

Cat flinched. "Sorry. I didn't mean that. I hurt your feelings. You really love your planet."

He pinned her with his gaze. "Now who is delving into whose mind?"

Her eyes widened and her mouth gaped. "Shit. Did I really do that?" She slapped a hand to her mouth. "I didn't mean to. It just happened."

"You're a natural."

She shook her head so hard her curls swung around her head. "Trust me. I'm not a natural at anything but music. I'm not good at math or science or even at making towels into swans."

He wrinkled his brow at her. "I do not understand 'towel' or 'swan' or how you could make one into the other."

She grinned at him. "Long story but trust me when I tell you I'm not a natural at mind reading. I've never even been very good with people before. You can ask Cassidy Bowen if you don't believe me. No, this is all about you and Trek."

Dev wrenched his gaze from her and patted the jebel who was shifting from one foot to the other. "It does not matter. We have promised to close our minds from yours. We have also promised to help you get back to your crew."

"Right."

Even though he'd walled off his mind from hers, he sensed disappointment in her voice, which confused him. Weren't they doing what she wished?

"Do those things sleep standing up?" she asked after the jebel grunted and stomped his feet.

"No, but he's still agitated from the swarm. It might take him a while to unwind enough to sit down and sleep."

Cat crossed behind him and stood on the other side of the jebel, resting her hand on the tuft of fur on top of his head. Before the animal could shake her off, she started to sing.

The jebel and Dev were so startled by the high, sweet sound that they both froze. The notes carried across the night air, entrancing both of them. After a few moments, the jebel bent one knee and then the other, sinking down onto the sand. As the final notes of her song drifted away, he bent his head and nestled his chin into his wattle, his eyes closed and his breathing heavy.

"You sang him to sleep," Dev whispered.

Cat shrugged. "Like I said, it's the one thing I do well. The one thing I love to do."

"I don't need to enter your mind to know that. I could feel it in the song."

She gave the jebel and final gentle pat. "It was a lullaby my gran used to sing me. I guess it reminds me of a time I was happy."

With that, she turned and walked back into the tent. Dev flopped back onto the sand next to the jebel, his chest tight. He couldn't remember the last time he'd felt so completely at peace and heartbroken at the same time. How could he let her go when his heart ached and told him she was meant to be his?

CHAPTER
ELEVEN

Cat's legs were shaky as she walked toward the tent and purposefully didn't glance back at Dev. What the hell was that?

It wasn't that she'd felt his mind delving into hers. She hadn't. It was her who'd sensed him and pulled his thoughts to her like a warm blanket that she'd wanted to drape over her shoulders. She'd sensed his longing for her, but it hadn't been as much of a pounding desire as a familiar hum of need. When she'd sung, his longing had almost become wistful and sad, so much so that her throat had thickened, and she'd had to turn from him before she did something crazy.

She stumbled into the tent and let the flaps close behind her. Trek sat cross-legged with a pair of glowing light sticks crisscrossed on the animal skin in front of him.

He put a finger to his lips. "Don't tell Dev. He hates it when I use Crestek gadgets."

"Crestek?" The word sounded familiar, but she forgot what it meant.

His face twisted for a beat. "They live on the other side of the planet where the sands become rocky peaks. We used to be one people, then we were enemies, and now we are learning to be allies and friends."

"And here I thought you were a desert planet with a few scattered tents," she said with a shake of her head, as she sat down across from him and crossed her own legs. At least thinking of the alien planet would take her mind off the alien outside who'd stirred something in her.

Trek straightened, looking affronted. "We are more than a ball of sand, as you put it."

"I know. I'm sorry. I didn't mean anything by it. I haven't been to any planets but Earth, so this is all new to me."

"I thought you were a space explorer journeying on a ship with advanced technology."

Cat tried not to laugh at this description. She was about the farthest thing from a space explorer as there was. "It's true the ship is sophisticated. I didn't lie about any of that. It's one of the newest ships in a fleet of star cruisers, but I'm not much of a space traveler. This was my first trip, and I tricked my way onto the crew. I'm pretty clueless when it comes to space and ships, which is why my escape pod ended up landing so far off course."

Trek scooted closer, his face alight. "You must have some interest in adventure, or you never would have gone to such lengths to get a position on the ship."

"More like I needed a job badly, and once you have an in with one of these space liners, you're set. They pay well plus you get room and board on the ship, and even though it isn't in one of the fancy suites the passengers enjoy, it's still nicer than anyplace I've lived before. But most of all, it meant job security and not having to wonder how I was going to survive from one week to the next. And after hacking it on my own for so long, it was nice to be a part of a crew. I even made friends." Her gut clenched at the thought of Maya and how she was probably worrying.

"I understand why you want to return so badly."

Cat lifted her gaze to meet his. "You do?"

He bobbed his head up and down. "My brother knows this, so it is no secret between us, but I long to travel among the stars. As much as I love our home world and what the sands have taught me, I know that my place is above."

"You said there are other Dothveks who live on a ship, right?"

Trek's lips thinned. "Our kinsmen found mates with a female bounty hunter crew that was marooned here, and they returned with them to the skies to continue hunting bounties."

"That sounds adventurous. You can't join them?"

He lifted his chin and made a clicking sound in his throat, his gaze fixed on the glowing sticks. "Not yet."

Cat sensed that he wasn't telling her everything, but she quickly reminded herself that she wasn't supposed to creep into their heads if she didn't want them in hers. She wrapped her arms around her knees and pulled them to her chest as a light breeze fluttered through the flap she hadn't tied closed. "Life on a ship is different from life on an open planet like this. For one, there are no animals to ride."

Trek shrugged. "My brother is the one with an affinity for and talent with beasts. He is the hunter who can lull his prey so fully that they nearly leap into his sack. My interests do not lie with smelly animals."

Cat grinned. So, she wasn't the only one who'd thought the alien camel thing had reeked. "No?" She shouldn't care about this alien and what captured his fancy. She would be leaving soon, and there was no point in learning about aliens she would never see again. But she couldn't help herself. "What are your interests?"

He looked at her, his dark slash of eyebrows lifting before the words spilled from him. "I like to know how things work." He waved a hand at the glowing sticks. "Like these. When I first saw them, I had to take them apart to know how they worked. Technology is like magic when you don't understand it, and I love to unravel the magic."

"Then you would love the star cruiser. They have replicators for food and holodecks for entertainment."

He wrinkled his nose. "I do not know either of these words."

"A replicator is a machine that transforms regular energy into matter so you tell the machine what you want to eat, and it will make it for you instantly."

"A machine creates food from nothing?"

"Nothing can be made from nothing," Cat said. "I wasn't a star student in physics, but I do remember that much. The machine uses energy to make matter."

Trek nodded slowly as if digesting this. "And the holodeck?"

"More energy into matter, although on a holodeck the matter becomes any surrounding you program." She waved a hand around them. "I could program the holodeck simulation to look exactly like this tent and then visit it whenever I wished."

Now his eyes were wide. "Would you do that?"

She couldn't stifle her laugh. "Probably not. For one, as crew I get almost no holodeck time and I don't know If I'd want to revisit the place where I hid from a swarm of insects."

Trek joined her in smiling. "I would not want to revisit the sands once I got away and onto a ship."

"You never know. You might be homesick one day."

He considered this as he scooted closer to her. "This is true, and there are some good things about this tent I would not mind remembering."

Cat's heart fluttered in her chest and heat pulsed between her legs. Wait, she felt something for this brother, too? Although the sensations were different, there was no doubt that she was attracted to both twins. She guessed that made sense. They were huge and gorgeous and looked alike, but she couldn't have a thing for both of them. Could she?

CHAPTER
TWELVE

Trek had promised not to enter the human's mind, but he hadn't promised not to talk to her. And if talking led them to the furs, that would not be the worst thing, would it?

His brother might think so, but Dev had chosen to leave the tent and stay outside with the jebel. Could Trek help it if his older brother preferred the company of beasts? He certainly did not, and he would not be nagged by guilt if the female chose him to take to her furs instead of Dev.

The fact that both he and his brother had sensed her thoughts and that she had been able to read theirs was unsettling. They knew about mind mates—all Dothveks did. Now, they even knew that it was possible for an off-worlder to be a Dothvek's mind mate. But Trek was still not certain he believed the myths about twins sharing a mind mate. He was not sure if he and Dev could share something as valuable as this.

Cat cleared her throat, her cheeks pink. "Holodecks can recreate anything or anyone as long as you can imagine it. I'm sure you could think of something or someone you would want to create more than this tent."

This holodeck technology sounded like something he would want to see from the inside out, but at the moment he couldn't imagine wishing himself from the tent and the human whose breath had quickened. "There is no one I would create who could match you."

She laughed at this, the sound high and nervous. "I've heard a lot of lines, but that's a good one."

"Lines?" Another word he did not understand.

"You know, something a guy says to a girl to get her to go out with him."

"I do not wish to go outside the tent with you." He shifted his body until their knees were brushing. "I wish to stay right here."

"No, it means..." She licked her lips. "You're saying nice things to make me like you and want to..."

His heart thudded in his chest. If Dev couldn't sense his desire, he would soon be able to hear the pounding of his heart. "I am only saying what is true, but are these truths making you like me?"

"I already liked you," she said, then sucked in air, as if the words had escaped without her wishing to say them.

Trek uncrossed his legs and widened them, moving forward to bend them around her. "I like you, but you probably didn't need me to tell you." He took her hand in his, turning it over and placing the pad of his thumb on her fluttering pulse. "You could sense it just as I can sense your desire."

She shook her head weakly. "I haven't gone into your..."

"I know," he whispered, lifting her wrist and brushing his lips across the soft skin. "But it doesn't take a mind meld to sense how much I want to take you to the furs."

Her eyes flitted to the pile of furs and blankets to one side. "But I just met you. I barely know you."

The tremble in her voice belied her nerves and the untruth in her words. "It doesn't feel like you just met me, does it? It feels like you've known me for much longer, doesn't it?"

A breath hitched in her throat, and she nodded. "It doesn't make sense, but I do feel like I already knew you. Like I've known you for a long time." She hesitated for a beat. "Both of you."

Trek paused. She felt the same way about Dev. He didn't know why he should be surprised by this. They'd found the female together, saved her together, and she'd picked up both of their thoughts and sent her own into both of their heads. It was clear that she was drawn to them as a pair.

As close as he was to his older brother and as many things as they'd shared over their lifetimes, they'd never shared a female. Not at the same time, at least. There was not an abundance of Dothvek females, so they had both bedded the same priestesses. But never on the same night and never together.

"Tell me what you want, Catarina." Trek ran a finger down the side of her cheek. "If you tell me you wish to sleep alone on the furs, I will leave you. If you tell me you wish me to join you, I will eagerly be your fur mate this night. If you wish to take my brother to the furs, I will step aside. What is it you want?"

Her pupils were so wide they made her dark eyes appear black as her breathing became shallow. She bit her lower lip, pulling it up in her teeth. Before she could give him an answer, the tent flaps rustled, and Dev stepped inside.

He glanced at the two of them and frowned. "Brother?"

Trek felt called out even though he was not in the wrong. "I have asked her to choose. She can choose either one of us or neither."

"I know." Dev's fiery expression shifted to the female. "She summoned me to the tent."

Trek jerked as if stung. She'd summoned his brother? How had he not sensed this?

Maybe because your desire is overpowering your abilities, and even your reason, a stern voice in the back of his head told him.

Disappointment washed over him, dousing his carnal hunger, and filling him with the need to run far from the tent. His shoulders sagged, and he dropped her hand. "You choose Dev. I understand."

She smiled at him, even though the edge of her lips quivered. "You don't understand."

Trek stood quickly and crosses to the tent flaps. "I might be the younger twin, but I am no fool, and I do not wish to remain and be a spectator."

Cat stood, matching his speed, and catching his hand before he ducked between the flaps. "I don't want you to be a spectator." Then she took Dev's hand in her other. "I want you both—together."

CHAPTER
THIRTEEN

Cat trembled as she held their hands and the two aliens stared down at her. She'd just told them she wanted them both—at the same time—and they hadn't said a word. Even their thoughts were inscrutable, a muddle she couldn't untangle.

What are you doing? The timid voice was barely a whisper above the rushing of blood in her ears and the crashing of her heart against her ribs.

What was she doing? This was insane. She had just met them, even if what she'd admitted was true. She felt like she'd known them for so much longer. There was an inexplicable familiarity about the aliens that made no sense. She'd never felt this comfortable with any human men, even ones she'd known for years. But with Dev and Trek there was something she'd never felt before—something deeper. As crazy as it was—and she knew just how crazy it was—she wanted to explore what it was between them.

But you're leaving, the chirpy voice reminded her.

She was leaving. Hadn't that been her entire goal—to find a way off the planet and back to her crew? Then what did it matter? If she was leaving and would never see them again, even better. If this was a colossal mistake, she'd never have to see them again or deal with the fallout of a stupid decision. But it didn't feel stupid. It felt oddly right.

"Did you say you want us both?" Dev asked, his voice husky.

"Together?" Trek added, glancing at his brother.

Even though nerves were swirling in her stomach, she nodded. "That's right. I don't want to choose one of you over the other, and I don't want to wait."

What the hell has happened to me? Cat's cheeks flamed as she wondered if maybe it was the planet's goddess energy that was turning her into such a wanton woman. Even if it was, she didn't care. She'd had to abandon ship, she'd crashed onto a desert planet, and she'd been chased by a bug swarm. If anyone deserved to burn off some stress with a couple of gorgeous, built aliens, it was her.

Trek growled low and tugged her toward the furs, but Dev held tight to her hand.

"We should set some rules," he said.

Trek's growl became impatient. "Brother."

Cat's heart stuttered as she looked up at Dev. His eyes were molten as they held hers, and her knees wobbled. She'd agree to any rule he wanted.

"If we do this, then we have free rein with your mind as well as with your body," he said, his gravelly voice rumbling through her. "I want to be free to explore all of you."

She finally released her breath. It was hard to imagine she'd have the energy or focus to explore their minds, but turnaround was fair play. "Agreed. And the same goes for both of you. If you get to read minds, so do I."

Now Dev growled as he tangled a hand in her hair and tipped her head back. "Do you really want to know all my dark desires, Catarina?"

"I want all of you," she said, meeting his possessive gaze.

His lips quirked into a half smile before he crushed his mouth to hers. She was consumed by the passion of his kiss and the surprising softness of his lips as his mouth moved dominantly against hers. When he parted her lips with a deft move of his tongue, she was reminded again that these brothers weren't the brutish barbarians she'd first assumed they were.

Even as she sank into Dev's kiss, Cat was aware of Trek's body and hands behind her. He was pressed up to her, his hands moving down her body and curling around her waist, his fingers dipping under her shirt and her bra. When he found her nipples, she drew in a sharp breath.

Dev moaned in her mouth, and she was vaguely aware of the brothers' exchanging thoughts in their mind. When she realized that they were telling each other what they were doing to her, desire arrowed through her so powerfully her body jerked. She hadn't imagined how hot it would be to hear two men talking about her.

Her breasts are so round and perfect, brother. I cannot wait for you to touch them.

Dev kissed her more deeply, sliding his hands down to cup her ass. *Will you watch me while I touch her?*

Gladly, brother.

Cat's knees buckled, but the two aliens were holding her up with their bodies. Trek rolled her pebbled nipples between his fingers, making her pussy clench with desire as Dev continued to kiss her and use his grip on her ass to press her into the hard bar of his cock. Fuck, she wanted to take off her clothes and get onto the furs.

You heard the female, Dev said, as Trek slipped his hands from her breasts and began to unfasten her pants. Soon, he was sliding them and her panties over her hips and down the length of her legs. Then he ran his hands up her bare legs as he stood, letting out a guttural noise as he pulled her shirt up and over her head, breaking her kiss with Dev for a moment. But Dev only caught a quick breath before setting his mouth on hers again as Trek worked the clasp of her bra and then slid her arms from it.

She is a goddess, Trek told his brother, when she was completely naked.

A goddess who needs to be worshipped, brother. Dev used his knees to spread her legs and then grabbed her hips and angled her ass up.

Before she could wonder what he was doing, Trek was on his knees, flipping himself so he was facing up, and his hot tongue was parting her from behind while Dev held her open to him.

Trek lapped at her, sliding his tongue in and out. Then the tip of his tongue found her clit, and she rocked her hips into him with a gasp.

She tastes like the sweetest honey. Trek circled her clit with his tongue, sending pleasure ricocheting through her. *Do you want a taste?*

You have your fill, brother. Then I will feast while you watch.

Trek laughed, and the vibrations sent more ripples of pleasure through her. *If I can resist filling her with my cock before then.*

Dev snatched his lips from hers, moving his mouth down to her breasts, sucking on first one nipple and then the other as Trek continued sucking her clit. Soon the intensity of two mouths was more than she could handle, and pleasure exploded within her body, she legs trembling and jerking as she screamed and fisted her hands in Dev's hair.

PRIZE

When she was panting, Dev tore his mouth from her, his gaze both tender and plundering as his eyes peered up and held hers. "She doesn't want you to wait, brother."

CHAPTER
FOURTEEN

Dev's heart thundered like jebel hooves across the sands as he met the female's gaze. Her desire was as easy to read on her face as it was to hear storming through her head. She wanted them—both of them—and her rush of euphoria only hastened her desire.

When he'd joined her and Trek in the tent, Dev had been unsure of what he would find. He'd sensed her growing arousal, but he'd also sensed her beckoning him, her mind sending out a tendril of longing like a finger crooking him toward her. He'd been willing to cede her to Trek if that was what she'd wished, but that hadn't been what she'd wanted at all.

As soon as his lips had claimed hers and Trek had begun running his hands over her body, something had shifted in all of them. It was as if they'd all aligned to each other in perfect harmony with Trek and Dev moving in tandem like they'd always done. Her raw lust pounded through him and swirled with his own and with Trek's until Dev didn't know where their desires left and his began.

"You don't wish to claim her first, brother?" He spoke the words out loud, the deep sound reverberating around them. "You haven't tasted her yet."

Cat took a shuddering breath and ran a hand down Dev's bare chest, her fingers bumping over the ridged muscle. "Maybe it's my turn to taste."

Then she tugged at the waist of his pants until they slipped past his hips, and his hard cock sprung up as it was released from the strict constraints of the animal skin. Dev groaned as she took the base of his cock in her small hand, her fingers curling around his rigid flesh.

"So, you don't only have ridges on your back?" She eyed the raised rings around his cock, her eyes flaring with fascination.

Dev didn't know much about other species, but he'd heard that human males did not have ridges anywhere, a fact he found startling. He suspected a cock without raised ridges would be much less pleasurable for the females, and he savored the feel of her fingers as she bumped them along his ridges and licked her lips.

Trek had stepped back and was watching Cat touch his brother, but there was nothing awkward about it. It was like Trek was an extension of himself, and he sensed his younger brother's pleasure buzzing through him almost as powerfully as his own. And Trek was enjoying watching the female touch him. When Cat bent and took Dev's cock between her lips, it was Trek who moaned first.

Dev met his brother's gaze as Cat took the crown of his cock in her mouth and swirled her tongue around it. *Sons of the goddesses, her mouth is amazing.*

Trek dropped his gaze to where her lips were stretching over first one raised ring and then another. *She's taking you well.*

Dev rolled his head, the sensation of her hot, wet mouth sending frissons of pleasure dancing across his skin. He wound his fingers into her dark curls as she moved her mouth up and down his length. *She's ready to take you now.*

Trek's gaze shifted from her mouth—eagerly sucking his brother's cock—to her bare ass. She was not kneeling, only bending at the waist, so he positioned himself behind her and grabbed her hips. Yanking his own pants down, his cock jutted out thick and rigid from his body.

Cat continued to work her mouth up and down Dev's shaft making soft moaning sounds, but when Trek spread her legs and dragged the crown of his cock through her slickness, her moans deepened.

Dev fisted his hands in her hair, the vibrations from her moaning making him almost lightheaded. It was almost too much to watch her suck him and see his brother on the verge of claiming her. He closed his eyes for a beat and surrendered to the sensations, while also fighting the release that was racing to overwhelm him.

He knew the moment his brother started to push inside her. Cat let out a throaty moan that hummed around his cock, and Trek groaned.

She's so tight, brother.

Dev's cock twitched as if he was the one impaling her, and Cat took him even deeper into her mouth. Instead of being overwhelmed by them—and by taking them both at once—he sensed her rush of power. She loved the feeling of having them both.

"She wants more of you," Dev said, saying it out loud so Cat was sure to hear him.

She cast her eyes up, meeting his and moving her head up and down ever so slightly. Trek held his brother's eyes, his own dark with barely restrained frenzy.

Dev bit his own lip as Cat sucked him. *She wants everything you can give her, brother.*

Trek returned his gaze to the female, driving himself in until he was buried to the root. Then he held his cock inside her, as she twitched her ass and moaned around Dev's shaft.

I didn't think such a small creature would be able to take me. Trek palmed her ass cheek, letting out a low growl and squeezing. *But she took all of me.*

Dev tightened his grip on her hair. *She's taken both of us as if she was born to.* He felt a pulse of pleasure that wasn't his own. *And she loves it.*

Trek started to move in and out with long strokes, dragging his cock almost entirely out before driving it back in. Each time Cat moaned and sucked Dev harder. *Tell me about her mouth, brother, and I will tell you what it's like to be inside her.*

You will like the way she sucks your cock as if it is something delicious to be devoured.

Trek ran his tongue over his lip, his gaze riveted on Dev's cock disappearing into the female's mouth. *It's like I can feel her tongue and her tight heat squeezing me.*

Dev watched his brother fuck the female, but he felt no jealousy, only the pleasure that they were all feeling together. Her torrent of arousal was overpowering, though, and it took all his willpower not to explode.

Trek pulled him from his concentration with a single phrase. *She wants you to have a turn fucking her, brother.*

CHAPTER
FIFTEEN

There was no way Cat should have been loving it as much as she was. No way that taking two guys should fill her with as much of a feeling of power. But it did. Instead of feeling like she was being used, Cat felt like she was the one who was powerful. She could give them both pleasure so intense that it practically vibrated her bones.

When she'd first seen Dev's cock, she hadn't been sure she could take it in her mouth. Not only was it long and thick but it had raised rings going down the length of it. But Cat liked the feel of the cock ridges as her lips bumped over them. The feel of the ridges in her mouth was nothing compared to how incredible they felt inside her.

Cat might not have gotten a look at Trek's cock, but it felt just as huge as Dev's, and the raised rings rubbed her in all the right ways. With every thrust inside her, his ridges stretched and caressed her flesh, making stars dance in front of her eyes.

As she sucked Dev's cock, one hand splayed on his *V* of ridges below his stomach and the other fisting the base of his cock, his body was tight. Cat could sense the desire barreling through him but also how much he wanted to keep it in check. But she didn't want him to hold himself back. She wanted to feel all of him and all his passion, as wild and untamed as it might me. She wanted him to fuck her, as well as Trek.

Almost as soon as the thought had occurred to her, Trek held himself deep, panting. Then he leaned over her, his voice a dark purr. "You want my brother to take a turn."

A momentary burst of embarrassment made her cheeks heat but then she shook it off. She *did* want Dev to fuck her. She needed to take both of them. Cat nodded quickly.

"Say it," Dev growled. "Tell me what you want."

Her breath stuttered in her chest as she released Dev's cock from her mouth, wiping the corner of her lips. "I want your cock inside me."

Another growl as Trek pulled out and Dev walked behind her. But if she'd been expecting Trek to take Dev's place, she was wrong. Trek spun her so that she was facing the tent pole then he raised her arms over her head and pressed them to the wood.

"What if she tries to escape?" Dev asked.

Cat swung her head around, but before she could protest that she had no reason to run from them, Trek had pulled some of the tent pole rope down and bound her wrists to the pole. She jerked at the ropes, but they held tight. A thrill shot through her as the two alien warriors stood behind her while she was tied up and completely at their mercy.

Strong hands grabbed Cat's hips and pressed the small of her back so that her ass tilted up. She dropped her head between her shoulders as a broad crown teased her opening. She didn't know which of the brothers was about to fuck her, and she liked not knowing. Cat closed her eyes and bit down on her lip as he stroked into her.

Once he'd filled her to the hilt, Cat knew it was Dev. It

wasn't that his cock felt different—they were identical twins, after all—but he moved differently than Trek. He was more forceful and controlled, each thrust taking her breath away. She groaned as each ridge of his cock entered her, the hardness sending shockwaves through her.

You were right, brother. I've never felt something so tight and perfect. Dev's thoughts came to her almost as clear as words.

It's like she was made for us.

Cat gasped, hearing their thoughts about her making flames lick at her skin.

She likes that. Dev's laugh was a dangerous rumble. *Just like she loves taking our cocks.*

Then thick fingers stroked between her legs, quickly homing in on her clit and circling it deftly. Cat was filled and stretched to her limit as Dev thrust deeply, but just as her pussy started to quiver, he was gone.

She jerked her head up to protest, but then Trek was inside her. She gasped at the sudden intrusion, but he was thrusting so hard and fast she didn't have time to speak or think. Cat barely remembered how to breathe as he took over from where his brother had left off. His fingers slipped on her slick skin as he gripped her hips, sliding one hand around to roll the pad of his finger over her clit.

"Trek, Dev," she gasped, their names mingling on her tongue as easily as they'd taken turns filling her.

Pleasure consumed her, fierce and hot as Trek drove himself deep and she felt Dev's gaze on her. She craned her neck to see him watching her hungrily, like a predator waiting his turn to devour a helpless creature. But she was anything but helpless.

"You like having us both, don't you?"

Nodding her head seemed like admitting a deep, dark secret that should be whispered about and never said out loud.

"Say it," Dev ordered. "Tell us what you like."

Cat rolled her head back, letting her eyelids flutter as she shook her head. Her pulse spiked and her body trembled in surrender, her release unraveling her slowly, and then the tremors making her entire body clench around Trek like a vise. Her fingers dug into the wooden pole as she spasmed with a scream, Trek pistoning hard before his own release and a loud roar. Before her pulsing ceased, Trek had pulled out.

Dev's low laugh was velvety and dangerous as he took over, stroking inside and holding himself. Cat's twitching pussy coaxed a desperate groan from him, but he didn't remain motionless for long.

"I want to hear you tell me that you love having both of us as much as we love sharing you," he husked.

Cat felt drugged as she twisted to gaze at him. His gold skin glistened in the dim light; his muscles taut as his eyes held hers in a possessive lock that made her heart stutter. Beside him, Trek watched with rapt attention, as if he'd never seen anything as magnificent in his life. She thrilled with the thought that even though she was tied to the pole, she held the two huge aliens in thrall.

"I love it," she purred. "I love having both of your cocks. I love you sharing me." Then she whispered her darkest fantasy. "I love being your toy."

Dev grunted, his eyes flashing hot with need. "You are one toy I do not mind sharing with my brother—as long as I get my turn."

Then he bent over her, ran a hand up her neck and pulled her mouth to his in a hard, claiming kiss as he pulsed hot inside her.

CHAPTER SIXTEEN

Trek nuzzled his face into her mane of hair, coiling his arm around her waist to hold her flush to him as they slept. He groggily opened his eyes. Cat was sleeping with her back to him so that he was cocooning her from behind and Dev slept facing her, his arm under her head like a pillow. They were all naked and lying on top of the furs, just like they'd been last night when they'd collapsed in exhaustion, all sweaty limbs and heaving chests.

Memories of being inside her sent fresh pulses of desire through him, and his cock thickened. He instinctively moved his hand from his waist until he'd cupped one of her breasts, absently thumbing her nipple until it pebbled.

"You're insatiable," Cat murmured, swatting his hand away and rolling forward so that she was tucked into Dev's chest. His brother draped a possessive hand over her hip and opened one eye, giving Trek a half smile.

Trek rolled his eyes. His brother could pretend to be asleep, but he was not dead. Waking up in bed next to a beautiful, naked female would send arousal arrowing through any hot-blooded Dothvek. And after they'd found a female who would take them both? Trek would be happy if they could stay in bed forever and pretend the outside world didn't exist. Or at least if they could go a few more times before leaving the tent.

She needs to rest, Dev told him.

Trek sighed, doing a bad job of hiding his impatience and his arousal.

Cat rolled back and grinned at him. "She needs to walk."

"Did we hurt you?" Dev asked before he could.

Cat shook her head as she pushed herself onto her elbows. "It's not a bad hurt, but I'm a little sore." Her cheeks turned a faint shade of pink. "I'm not used to..."

"Two cocks?" Trek finished for her, his gaze skimming her body. "You took us like you'd been born for it."

The flush on her cheeks darkened. "I'm not sure if that's a good thing."

"It is for us," Dev said. "We've never found a female who could meld with both our minds."

Trek reached for her. "Or take both of us."

"So, you've never...?" She let her words trail off.

"Never," Dev said. "There is Dothvek lore of twin warriors taking a single mind mate, but it happened so long ago—if it isn't legend—that no one remembers."

Trek trailed a hand down the swell of her hip. "We didn't know it was possible until you arrived."

Cat's warm flurry of emotions stilled. "Mate?"

"Females who can connect to our minds and our bodies are not common among our people, even though we are empathic. Not every partner will be a mind mate," Dev said. "And not all mind mates must be Dothvek."

"So, you can have a mind mate who isn't one of your own kind?"

Trek rubbed the rough pad of his thumb over the softness

of her skin. "We didn't know we could until the bounty hunter females arrived. None of them were Dothvek and they were able to find their mind mates among the Dothveks."

"And Crestek," Dev added.

"I'm not exactly sure what all that means, but I can't be your mate if mate means even close to what I think it means."

Trek paused his movement, his hand frozen on her hip. "After last night, I thought..."

Cat stood quickly, pulling a blanket with her, and wrapping it around her chest. "Last night was amazing. Really amazing, but that doesn't mean anything changed. Not really."

Trek's throat tightened as he looked at her. The confident, bold female who'd been so uninhibited with them now seemed nervous and scared.

"I still have to return to my crew and my job," she said. "I might not be great at it, but it's my only way to make something of my life. I can't stay here no matter how much fun I might have had with you two."

Trek couldn't meet his brother's gaze. He could sense the disappointment wash over him as completely as it was engulfing him. He could also sense Cat's mind closing off to them, her feelings now only a distant hum behind a thick wall.

"I'm sorry if I gave either of you the impression that sex would change things. I thought we all were looking for some fun and stress release after everything that happened. If I ever led you on, I'm so—"

"You made us no promises," Dev said, standing abruptly. "If we dared to hope, that was our mistake."

Trek gaped at his brother. Why was he giving up so easily? How could he accept her rejection without trying to convince her that her place was with them?

Mind mates cannot be forced, brother.

Dev's sharp words stung him, but he knew the truth of

them. They'd seen the trials that their kinsmen had gone through with their own off-worlder mind mates. It could not be forced, and often their kinsmen had to nearly lose them before finally being united.

He eyed his brother as the Dothvek snatched his pants from the ground and tugged them on. Was he only appearing to agree with the female because he hoped she would find her way back to them or did he truly believe they should let her go? For one of the few times in his life, Trek did not understand his brother's mind.

Cat also watched Dev as he dressed hurriedly. "I never meant to lead anyone on or hurt you—either of you."

"We are not untested warriors, Catarina." Dev paused at the flaps of the tent. "We have survived worse."

Then he walked out, leaving me naked with her. She gnawed on her bottom lip nervously, and I could sense the sadness in her even through her barriers.

Even though I was usually the brother accused of being rash and impulsive, this time it was Dev who'd acted too quickly. There was regret in her, and not regret about what we'd done. Regret for having to part with us. She wasn't as eager to go as she might want us to believe.

"Do not let Dev bother you," I said, standing and stretching and relishing the long, lingering look she gave me. "You cannot blame him for missing you already."

Cat gave me a shy smile and then began to gather her own clothes that were strewn around the tent. "Thanks."

I made a point to take my time in pulling on my pants. I wanted her to believe that I was taking her rejection in stride. "Don't worry. We will still take you to the Crestek city so you can send a transmission to your crew."

Her head snapped up and her blanket slipped from under her arms and pooled at her feet. "You will?"

"That's your best chance of getting back to your ship quickly, isn't it?" I crossed to her, keeping my gaze trained on her face and not on her lush, naked body. "We promised to help you and we will. That hasn't changed."

Then I bent down and brushed a kiss across her lips before walking from the tent. Despite her best efforts to hide her emotions, I picked up her pleasant surprise—and another pang of regret. My plan was already working.

CHAPTER SEVENTEEN

Dev scowled at his brother across the swaying wattle of the jebel as they walked on either side. Cat rode on the back of the beast, her head draped with white fabric to keep the sun from burning her, but he and Trek had chosen to walk. As fond as he was of jebels, he preferred the warm sand beneath his feet.

The two suns were rising higher over the dunes that stretched out in all directions, sending warm slats of light bursting over the glittering gold sand. The heat had not yet started to shimmer off the sand, but whatever creatures emerged in the cool of the night had scuttled back under the surface, their prints evaporating as the faint breeze spun a fine mist of sand. The only sounds were the rhythmic plodding of the jebels wide hooves on the sand. The Dothveks' footfall was silent, as they'd trained it to be when they moved across the dunes.

Tell me again why we're going to the Crestek city, brother.

Trek blew out a breath, casting a quick glance at the female even though they were masking their thoughts from her. *We promised to help her find her way back to her ship. The Crestek have the best way to do that.*

Dev's scowl deepened. *You wish to take our mate into the heart of enemy territory?*

They are no longer our enemies, remember? We were both there when the peace was forged.

Dev stroked a hand down the jebel's furry neck, memories of the battle and the truce fresh. He remembered agreeing to peace, but it was not so easy to shrug off generations of distrust so quickly.

I know, brother. Trek did not need him to tell him why the thought of entering the territory of their former enemy felt so wrong. *But we cannot keep her on the sands, as much as we might want to. She is not of our world.*

Dev jerked his head up. Maybe Cat was an off-worlder, but that didn't mean she couldn't adjust to their way of life. She'd already adjusted to their communication. If she could do that, wasn't she meant to be on their planet and with them? *But do we have to take her into their city? I still do not trust them, especially around a female—our female.*

Trek cocked an eyebrow. *I know they have not always been trustworthy around females, but the Cresteks are not all the same. Think of T'Kar. He is not a dishonorable Crestek.*

Dev grunted at the reminder of one of the bounty hunters' chosen mates, who happened to be a Crestek. *Yes, but he is different. He was a part of their underground resistance group, and he went through the* tahadu *to become a Dothvek. Now, he is one of us.*

Trek inclined his head as if acknowledging this. *How is it that I am the one speaking reason and understanding? Usually, you are the one to talk me down.*

We have never had a mind mate before.

The twins walked in silence for a few steps.

She is not ours if we force her to stay, Trek finally told his older brother. *She is only our mate if she chooses to be. You know that.*

Dev shot his brother a severe look. *You think I would force any female?*

No, although we both enjoyed seeing her tied up and at our mercy last night.

Heat stirred in Dev's core at memories of Cat naked and bound flooded his brain. He'd never been as aroused in his life as he'd been when she'd submitted to them both. *That was not by force. She wanted that as much as we did.*

Trek smiled, his gaze darting to the female riding above them. *I know. That is what made it so good. She wanted it. If she also wants to leave, we cannot stop her. We should not.*

Dev huffed out a breath, hating how much sense his younger brother made and despising him for being right. Of course, they could not keep Cat on their world if she wished to leave. He'd only hoped that melding with their minds and being such a perfect match for their bodies and their appetites would have made her want to stay. *When did you become the wise one, brother?*

Trek shrugged. *Maybe I've been paying more attention to you than you thought.*

Or maybe you've been hanging around Tommel and picking up his maddening wisdom. He cut a gaze to Trek. *Either way, I do not like it.*

Trek threw back his head and laughed, which caused Cat to give them both curious looks.

Trek cleared his throat and looked down, the corners of his mouth still quivering. "Apologies. I thought of an amusing story I heard."

Cat nodded, but Dev thought Trek was lucky that she didn't ask for details about the story. His brother clearly hadn't lost all his impulsive and reckless tendencies, which was some comfort.

I must admit something, Dev. Trek rested his own hand on the jebel's neck, absently stroking it as they walked. *My motive for taking her to the Crestek city is not entirely pure.*

Dev tilted his head to look at his brother. *Is this about your desire to know how our enemy's communication system works?*

Trek gave him a crooked grin. *No, although now that you mention it, that is another good reason.*

Dev gave him a pointed look, although he could not fault his brother for being curious. Since they were young, Trek had always been fascinated by taking things apart. It had led to many tents collapsing and an entire pen of jebels being inadvertently released.

By helping her get what she wants, she will see that she can trust us. If we do what we promised and aid her in getting back to her ship, even though we clearly want her to stay, then we will be making a sacrifice for her.

Maybe his brother really was losing his tendency to act first and then think. *You believe she will recognize this sacrifice as evidence of our feelings for her?*

Trek thumped the jebel's neck and nodded. *I do.*

And if she still chooses to leave after all this?

Trek held his gaze for a long beat. *Then she was never ours.*

Dev growled and faced forward again; his eyes trained on the dunes that extended from them like rolling waves. He hoped his brother was right, but he feared they were leading their mate from them and into danger.

CHAPTER EIGHTEEN

Cat jerked herself up before she slumped forward on the jebel. Crap! Had she started to drift off again? The plodding footsteps of the jebel combined with the heat under the white fabric draped over her head kept making her nod off. If she wasn't careful, she was going to fall asleep and fall right off the animal's back.

She readjusted herself on the blankets beneath her, flinching at the ache between her legs. Between the jebel ride and the night before, she'd be lucky if she could walk again.

When she peeked up from underneath the drape hanging over her forehead, blowing a breath up and fluttering the fabric, she was startled to see that the view was no longer endless, golden, sand dunes. The desert had given way to a mountain range, the craggy rocks the same golden hue as the sand, and just as shimmery.

She tipped her head up. "I did not see this coming."

"The Crestek city is beyond the rocks," Dev said, leading the jebel forward to a ledge and stopping it. "We'll have to go by foot the rest of the way."

As Dev coaxed the animal to bend first one knobby knee and then the other, Trek reached up and took hold of her waist as she swung one leg over to join the other. When she slid off the jebel's back, he continued to hold her waist for balance.

Trek's hands were warm and firm on her waist. "Can you walk, or would you like me to carry you?"

She answered quickly without thinking. "I'm not a child. I can walk."

He tilted his head, giving her a suggestive smile. "I thought you might be sore from the jebel, and from…"

Even though she was already warm, her cheeks heated. How did he know that? She narrowed her gaze at him. "Were you delving into my thoughts again?"

His smile instantly vanished. "No. I gave you my word I would not."

"You are not the first human female we had ridden jebels with across the sands," Dev said as he walked around the creature to stand with us. "We understand that riding them can be difficult if you aren't used to it."

"Oh." Cat felt like a jerk for accusing him of reading her mind when he was only being considerate. "Sorry. I am a little sore, but I'll be able to walk." Then she scrunched her lips to one side. "I'm not the first human female you've ridden jebels with but am I the…?"

"Yes." Dev didn't let her finish her question. "We have never been with another human woman."

"And we have never been with any female together," Trek added.

For some bizarre reason, that made Cat feel special. Not that it mattered. She would be hopping on a rescue ship soon, and the aliens would be nothing but a steamy memory. She shouldn't care who they'd done what with, or how often. It wasn't her business. Even so, she liked that she was the only one.

"Okay then." She attempted to wipe the grin from her face as she peered up at the high peaks, pulling the drape from her head and shielding her eyes from the sun. They looked remarkably dangerous and sharp, and mountain climbing was another thing she'd never attempted and didn't relish trying. "We have to go over these?"

"There is a path around the rocks and through them." Trek jumped onto the ledge and extended a hand to help her up while Dev slapped the jebel's rump and said a few words Cat didn't understand.

When the creature started to take off toward the sands again, she gasped. "You're letting it go?"

"It does not belong to us. It belongs to the sands." Dev watched the animal race up a dune, a cloud of sand puffing up behind it. "When we return to our village, we will not need it. We can run faster across the sands." He turned and met her gaze. "And you will not need it because you will be headed back to your ship."

Hearing him say that, even though it was exactly what she'd claimed she wanted, made her gut clench. "Right." She pivoted back to the mountains. "I guess we'd better do this."

Trek cut his eyes to the suns then to his brother. "We should be able to reach the city by the setting of the suns if we follow the path around."

"They will see us coming," Dev said, "but now that we are at peace, that should not matter."

Cat didn't like the way the Dothveks talked about these Cresteks. They might have brokered a peace with them, but it was clear that the twins didn't trust them. She was very aware that Dev didn't want to be entering the enemy territory. Even without delving into his mind, she could tell by the way he spoke of them, and the suspicion in his eyes. But he was doing this because of her.

She swallowed hard as Trek led the way through a crack in the rock, motioning for her to follow him, and Dev fell in step behind her. Light shone between the towering rock as they trekked in silence, the path not wide enough for them to walk three astride.

Cat flinched with each step, the ache between her legs making her wish she'd walked by the jebel like the Dothveks had. When she sucked in a quick breath, Dev wordlessly scooped her up in his arms.

"What are you doing?" she asked, although her protest was weak even to her own ears.

"It pains me to see you in pain, especially since it is partly my fault. I would rather carry you."

Trek glanced behind him, and his mouth quirked up before he turned back around.

Cat allowed herself to relax into Dev's broad chest. "It's not your fault. Well, not entirely. And that jebel isn't blameless."

He grunted at this, but she could tell he was amused.

She wound her arms around his neck and let her cheek press against his chest as they proceeded around the looming rock face, finally approaching high, stone walls. After the vastness of the desert and the primitive tent, she was stunned to see domes and spires peeking above the high barrier. "This is the Crestek city?"

Dev tensed. "This is the enemy's lair."

Cat shivered, almost afraid of what was beyond the ramparts, as they continued through the opening gates.

CHAPTER NINETEEN

Trek peered up at the massive, wooden gates as they walked through them and into the bustling Crestek city. The quiet of the sands and the solitude of the mountains were swallowed up by the cacophony of voices and lilting music spilling from high windows. Colorful fabric was draped above them in the air, and tall, stone buildings were topped with domes or peaks.

It was so unlike the oasis tent village that was his home that he swallowed hard and tried not to become overwhelmed by the size and noise. He'd been in the Crestek city once before—when the peace was brokered—but he hadn't ventured beyond the walls since.

"I had no idea your planet had a city like this," Cat said, her eyes wide with wonder. "It's almost like a regular outpost."

Dev grunted. "The Cresteks still do not openly welcome outsiders, so you will find no off-world traders or travelers here."

"Except me," Cat said.

Trek made a low noise in his throat as he noticed the

curious gazes swinging toward them and alighting on the human female. Some of the Cresteks were interested in them. Despite the peace, the two peoples remained different. While the Dothvek wore little clothing because they lived on the hot sands, their old enemy wore long cloaks that shielded them from the suns' rays. After retreating from the dunes so many generations ago, they no longer had the resistance to the harsh suns.

As Cresteks passed them, the long hems of their gray, blue, or white robes fluttering and dark eyes peering out from underneath their hoods, Trek tensed. Maybe this hadn't been a good idea. Maybe bringing Cat into their old enemy's city had been a tactical error.

I told you, Dev's voice was clear in his head. *This was a mistake.*

Trek was starting to agree with him. Maybe they could retreat and find some other way to contact the bounty hunters. Or they could convince Cat to be patient and wait for the ship's return.

Before he could tell Cat that they should leave, a Crestek female approached them in silvery robes that were made of a shimmery fabric instead of the usual thick one. She threw back her hood and appraised Cat openly before shifting her heavily lined eyes to the twins.

Trek sensed a flash of irritation from Cat. She didn't like the way the Crestek female eyed them. Then the Crestek smiled brightly.

"You are human, are you not?"

Cat stiffened but the Crestek was undeterred. She laughed, the high, chirpy noise carrying over the din of voices.

"Of course, you are. I saw one of your kind when she was mated to the old chancellor's son. I recognize your stature and your lack of ridges." She leaned closer. "I also can tell that you've had both of these Dothveks."

When Cat drew in a quick breath, the Crestek female laughed again and fluttered a hand in the air. "Do not think we mind such a thing. In fact, Crestek females take many lovers and sometimes multiple mates." She let her gaze linger on Trek and Dev again. "But the idea of twin Dothveks is very tempting."

"We are not here to acquire mates," Dev said gruffly.

The Crestek female stuck out her lower lip. "No? Too bad. Then why are you here?"

Trek curled his fingers around the hilt of his blade for comfort as he scanned the crowd that continued to cast them curious looks. "We are here to send a transmission."

Another sigh from the Crestek. "That isn't as exciting as I'd hoped." She twitched one shoulder up. "I'll take you to the communications hub. My brother Karv works there. He'll help you." She winked at them. "He's always been curious about Dothveks."

With that, she beckoned for them to follow her. Trek shot his brother a questioning look, but Dev only cocked his head, as if to ask if they had a better option. They snaked through the bustling square of the city, with Trek and Dev walking tightly in front and back of Cat, who continued to swivel her head and take in the market stalls and the imposing stone structures.

When they reached the base of a tall, tower-like building, the Crestek female. had a furtive conversation with a guard then she pivoted around to face them. "Here's where I leave you." Then she put a hand on Trek's arm and gave him a sultry smile. "If you change your mind, just tell Karv to find Linnea."

Before he could think of a polite response, Cat cleared her throat. "We won't change our minds but thank you."

The Crestek raised her dark slashes of brows slightly. "I

don't blame you one bit, human. If I had a pair of Dothveks like this to myself, I wouldn't want to share, either." Then she laughed as she spun around, her robes swirling, and waved a hand as she walked away. "But you can't blame me for trying."

Trek shifted uncomfortably. He'd heard the Crestek females were freer with their desires, and since there were fewer of them than there were males, they were given their choice of mates and often took more than one. He'd never experienced one first-hand, though.

"Are all the women on your planet like that?" Cat asked, after Linnea had left them.

Trek opened his mouth to explain the differences between Crestek and Dothvek females, but a Crestek male stepped from the door of the building. "Linnea, what...?" Then he took in the sight of them, and his mouth gaped. "I was told my sister had a gift for me."

Trek squared his shoulder at the Crestek in a blue robe with the hood pushed back. "I'm afraid it is only us. We are hoping to avail ourselves of the new peace between our peoples and send a transmission to our kinsman on the bounty hunter ship."

The male's face brightened. "Then my mischievous sister brought you to the right place. I am Karv, and I run the communications hub for the city." He gave them a small bow. "Please come inside and I can show you our communications facility and assist you in contacting your kinsmen."

Trek's pulse quickened at the thought of exploring the communications hub and discovering how their system worked. He stepped forward to join Karv, but his brother's heavy hand clamped over his arm.

"You send the transmission. I will find food for Catarina."

Trek hesitated. He'd been so caught up in his own excitement that he'd ignored the need he now sensed from her. Of course, she was hungry.

It is fine, brother. Do not worry. Send our transmission.

Trek slid his gaze to Cat, who grinned at him.

"Go on. We'll scrounge up some food."

Karv hesitated inside the doorway, turning back. "Are you coming?"

Trek turned to him then back to Dev and Cat, but they were already moving away and vanishing into the crowd. The muddle of so many thoughts was like a restless hum in the back of his mind, but he forced himself not to listen to them. There were too many. He suppressed a momentary burst of panic that they were surrounded by their former enemy before reminding himself that their peoples had made peace. The Cresteks no longer wished the Dothveks harm. At least, that was what he hoped.

He took a deep breath, and pivoted back to Karv. "I am ready."

CHAPTER
TWENTY

Dev rested one hand on Cat's hip as he steered her toward the Crestek open air market. He was drawn to the aroma of food as much as by the chattering of voices and tapping of feet on the paving stones.

It was impossible for them to blend in. He was a bare-chested Dothvek in a sea of cloaked Cresteks, and she was a human female considerably smaller than any native female on his planet. She also drew stares for her utilitarian pants and shirt. Crestek females were known to wear elaborate and revealing dresses underneath their cloaks, although he'd never seen this with his own eyes.

Dev's empathic abilities were overloaded with the sheer volume of minds surrounding him. The torrent of voices swirled around him, but he was able to keep them at bay while still picking up on Cat's emotions. She was also overwhelmed, but fascination was winning out over fear as they reached the multitude of stalls with canopies.

She paused at one vendor roasting some type of meat on a spit. "Is this food similar to yours?"

Dev's stomach rumbled as fat dripped off the slowly spinning meat and sizzled on the hot coals beneath. "Somewhat."

The female's hunger was as obvious as his, and they both must have appeared famished to the vendor who held out two wrapped bundles.

"With my compliments," the vendor said, pushing back his beige hood. "It isn't often we get new faces in the market."

Cat beamed at him, eagerly taking the wrapped food. "Thank you. It smells delicious."

"A Crestek specialty called swarka," the vendor said. "I hope you enjoy it."

Cat unwrapped hers quickly and bit into the end of the meat wrapped in a puffy flatbread, moaning softly as she chewed. "This is my new favorite food."

The Crestek's gold cheeks deepened in hue at this compliment. Dev took a bite of his own swarka, the savory flavor of the meat reminding him instantly of sitting around the fire at the oasis village. He inclined his head in thanks to the Crestek, as they moved along and chewed.

"Do the Dothveks eat swarka?" Cat asked.

"We have something very similar, although this is one of the better versions I have eaten."

Cat nodded absently as she devoured her food, and Dev couldn't help feeling a pang of guilt that she was so hungry.

"We should get something for Trek," Cat said, when she'd polished off her food and was dabbing at the corners of her mouth.

It heartened Dev that she thought of Trek, and he was even more pleased to know that he harbored no jealousy that she thought of his brother. Their connection to Cat was truly one they'd forged together, and there was no place for envy between them.

Cat spun around to return to the vendor, but her way was

blocked by several Crestek males in dark brown robes with their hoods back.

"We heard there was a pretty female walking around in the market," one of them said, blatantly running his gaze up and down Cat.

She backed up until she was flush against Dev. His hand instinctively went to his blade and his shoulders tensed. These Cresteks did not have the open, friendly faces of the others. These males looked at his female with a desire that made ire flare within him. "She is not alone."

The male who spoke for the other two flicked a dismissive gaze at Dev. "You are a stranger here, Dothvek."

"We are visitors." Cat's voice held an edge. "And we're together."

The Crestek glanced around. "I heard there were three of you. Where is the other Dothvek? Licking his wounds because he wasn't the chosen one?"

Cat crossed her arms over her chest. "Actually, I'm with both of them."

The Crestek's angled brows rose. "Then you're more like a Crestek female." Then he nudged his friends and laughed. "That works for us."

The crowd around them had backed up, the other Cresteks sensing the tension brewing as they murmured and shot furtive looks at Dev and Cat and the Crestek males.

"You should leave us," Dev growled. "I do not wish to fight you, but if you dishonor my mate with your comments, I will have no choice."

"Mate?" The leader slid his gaze to Cat. "You sure you want to be with one of those sand barbarians when you could have someone civilized?"

Dev's fingers coiled around the hilt of his blade, but Cat rested a hand on his arm. "I'm sure. Now my mate asked you to leave us alone. I suggest you listen to him." She smiled sweetly. "I'd hate for him to have to kick your ass."

The Crestek laughed at this. "I'd like to see him take all three of us."

Dev drew his blade and pushed Cat behind him. "Challenge accepted, Crestek."

Gasps and dark murmurs passed through the remaining crowd as an opening was formed. Vendors pulled back their wares and children were rushed away.

Dev did not want to engage in battle with the Cresteks, but their insults could not go unanswered. It was clear that not all Cresteks had abandoned their feelings about the Dothveks. Not everyone was ready for peace.

Maybe he was one of those who found it easier to slip back into old prejudices, Dev thought as he assumed a battle stance and the Crestek threw off his cloak. At least only one of the males was intending to fight him at once. He could take on three of them, but he preferred to dispatch them quickly one at a time.

The Crestek didn't carry a blade, but a knife was swiftly passed to him. He copied Dev's battle stance, but it was clear the Crestek had little experience fighting. Dev stole a quick glance at Cat who stood behind him, her face twisted in worry. He nodded at her as if to reassure her, and she managed to give him a weak smile. Then her eyes widened, and he turned quickly to see the other male rushing him.

Sidestepping the attack, Dev spun around and smacked the butt of his blade on the Crestek's back. The male stumbled but righted himself, his face gnarled with rage as he ran at Dev again. This time, Dev ducked the wild swing of his opponent's arm, catching the wrist and bending it back so that the Crestek flipped onto his back.

As the male crawled to his feet, Dev backed away and

waited for him to catch his breath. He had no desire to kill this Crestek or even seriously wound him, which was why he hadn't attacked with his blade. He only wished to wear him out and force him to admit defeat—and apologize for his words. "Do you wish to cease this fight?"

The Crestek's lip curled, and he charged again with a roar. Dev met his charge, grabbing the arm holding the knife and knocking it from his hand before plowing a shoulder into his chest and sending him staggering back and gasping for breath. The knife had clattered to the stones, and Dev scooped it up. Now that the male was disarmed, he would be forced to surrender.

He glanced again behind him to catch Cat's eye. But she was no longer behind him. He scanned the Crestek's gathered behind him, but she was not there. Panic twisted in his gut. She would not have left him in the middle of a fight. He scoured the market area, but there was no sign of her.

Then he looked back to his opponent, but the Crestek no longer stood across from him heaving in ragged breaths.

They were both gone.

CHAPTER
TWENTY-ONE

Cat's head was heavy as it lolled forward, and she jerked before she slumped fully. She blinked sluggishly, but her eyelids felt like lead. Forcing herself to open her eyes, she found her surrounding so dimly lit that she recognized nothing.

She wasn't in her quarters on the cruiser. She would have detected the ambient, lavender light inset in the ceiling. Wait, she'd left the cruiser. Memories of abandoning ship flooded back into her addled brain, followed by memories of landing on the sand planet and being rescued by the twin Dothveks.

Cat jerked upright before realizing she was sitting in a chair. Dev and Trek. Where were they?

She attempted to rub her temples, but she couldn't raise her arms. Her hands were bound behind her. She peered down at herself and saw that she wasn't in the clothes she'd been wearing. She wore some sort of dress made from sheer fabric; the top held up by thin shoulder straps. What the actual fuck?

She jerked at her ties, but they only rattled the chair. Squinting through the dim light, she calmed her racing mind.

The last thing she remembered was being in the Crestek city. She'd been with Dev in the market, they'd eaten something delicious, then there had been a fight. Her pulse fluttered as she remembered the jerks who'd accosted them, and then how valiantly Dev had fought the leader of the group. Then she'd felt a sting in her ass and things had gone sideways.

Cat shifted on the chair and the ass cheek she remembered getting stung ached from the pressure. She shifted back. Had someone jabbed her with a needle? Had she been drugged and then dressed up? Why? It wasn't like she knew anyone on the planet or had enemies.

A door creaked open, and a sliver of light hit her face. She flinched.

"You're awake." The male voice was unfamiliar.

"Who the hell are you, and why am I tied to a chair? Where are my clothes?"

The door was closed behind the speaker and darkness consumed the room again. "My name doesn't matter. You're tied up because we didn't think you'd come with us willingly or stay once you woke."

"Since I have no idea who you are or why you abducted me, you're right about that." Her grogginess had faded and was quickly replaced by outrage. "You didn't tell me why I'm not wearing my clothes."

"We thought it was more fitting for you to dress like a Crestek female if you're a guest in our city."

The thought that she'd been undressed while she was unconscious made her gut tighten, but she focused on my outrage. "I'm assuming you're Crestek."

"Since you are in the Crestek city, that's a safe guess."

"It's a safe guess, because Dothveks would never do something like this," she shot back. She may only know two Dothveks, but she knew enough about their sense of honor that she felt confident in her statement. And she wanted to insult the Cresteks who took her.

The male let out a low chuckle. "You have spirit. I'd heard that about human females."

"There are easier ways to learn about humans than by kidnapping them and dressing them like dolls."

"Maybe." He circled her, his face still in shadow. "Like I said, we didn't think you'd come willingly, and we didn't have to time to debate our options, once word got out that you were in our city with two Dothveks."

"This is all about your curiosity about humans?" Cat had never been on an alien world that didn't interact with other planets. Was she that much of a curiosity?

"Hardly, although you are intriguing. I can understand why the Dothveks desired you."

This made Cat squirm. She didn't like the way he was looking at her, the whites of his eyes visible in the dimness. Had he been the one to undress her? Bile teased the back of her throat, but she swallowed hard and took a deep breath.

"This is not about you. This is about the Dothveks," he continued. "Not all Cresteks are happy that a peace was forged between our peoples. Some of us preferred when we kept to ourselves. The Dothveks belong on the sands. They don't deserve to walk through our gates as if they haven't been our enemies for generations."

"Taking me is about punishing them?"

"In a way." His pace circling her increased, his shoes tapping the stone floor. "When the first human females arrived on our planet, it was the Dothveks who claimed them, aside from one Crestek, but he turned against his own kind and became one of them. Those barbarians should not get all the females who come to the planet."

Cat bit back the urge to suggest that they may run into

more crashed ships if they left their walled city, but she decided to stay silent. Why had she insisted on getting off the planet as quickly as possible? If she hadn't been so dead set on getting a transmission off, she might not be tied to a chair and held captive by Cresteks with a grudge.

She thought wistfully of the tent she'd shared with Dev and Trek. What she wouldn't give to be back there with both of them. Heat pulsed between her legs as she thought of being with both aliens. Would staying on the planet really be so bad? Not if she could count on more nights like that. The twin Dothveks were enough to make her forget her desire to return to the cruiser and have a secure, safe future.

Her heart lurched and she thought about Dev and Trek. Where were they now? They must have noticed her missing, and they must be in a panic.

"So, what's your plan? You're going to keep me here forever? I do have a ship that's looking for me, you know. The whole reason we came to your city was to send a transmission to my ship so I can be rescued."

The pacing stopped. "You aren't staying with the Dothveks?"

Cat felt traitorous saying that she intended to leave them, so she pressed her lips together. She'd told these abductors too much anyway.

The Crestek came up behind her and leaned down so that his breath tickled her ear. "If you like more than one male at a time, my friends and I would be more than happy to indulge you."

"No thanks. I'd rather wait for Dev and Trek to find me and wipe the floor with your sorry asses."

He ran a finger under one of the thin shoulder straps, pulling it down so that it dangled down the side of her arm.

"You aren't in much of a position to make demands, though, are you?"

Cat clenched her teeth so he wouldn't hear them chatter and know she was trembling. She just had to hold out until Dev and Trek found her. She hoped that would be soon.

CHAPTER
TWENTY-TWO

Trek stood next to Karv in the communications hub, his gaze trained on the dull-metal console. Located at the top of the building and reached by a ramp that spiraled up the interior, the room was ringed with consoles and windows overlooking the city. The antennae that transmitted the signals off-world extended from a central pole in the room that emerged from the ceiling onto the building's roof.

"Our transmission will be sent into space?" Trek's gaze shifted between the console and the metal pole.

Karv nodded. He'd shrugged off his cloak since they were the only ones in the room and wore a simple shirt and brown pants, so the two males didn't look so different anymore. "I set the message to repeat so it will loop until we receive a response. Even if your kinsmen's ship is far away, the message should travel far."

"You have possessed this technology for long?" Trek asked, marveling at the ability to send silent messages into the sky.

"It was augmented by the bounty hunters' own technology

so that they could communicate with this planet," Karv admitted. "Before, our technology was more basic."

"I'm surprised that your people welcomed technology that would bring interaction with other species," Trek said before he remembered what he was saying. "Not that I mean to insult your—"

Karv laughed it off. "No offense taken. You are right that there were many in the city opposed to progress or the peace. I was never one of them."

Trek raised a brow.

Karv glanced over his shoulder and lowered his voice even thought they were alone. "Before the peace, I was secretly part of the Crestek resistance."

Trek blinked at him. "You mean you wished to make peace with the Dothveks before it was generally accepted?"

Karv shoved one of his sleeves up to reveal a ring of dark tribal marks etched into his skin. "I am one of those who always revered the Dothvek ways. Part of me wished I was one of you."

"Long ago, we were one people," Trek reminded him. "That means we are technically still brothers."

Krav grinned at this, clearly pleased at the thought and Trek's openness. Loud footsteps made him quickly shove his sleeve back down as Dev burst into the room and they both spun to face him.

"Brother," Dev gasped, his expression wild.

Karv stared open mouthed. "Did you run up the entire way?"

Dev didn't answer, instead pinning Trek with an intense gaze.

"Where is Cat?" Trek asked, already dreading the answer, and knowing it deep in his soul.

"Gone." Dev scraped a hand roughly through his hair.

Karv's brow furrowed as he looked from one brother to the next. "The female who was with you?"

"Our mate." Trek locked eyes with Dev. "What do you mean gone?"

"We were in the market. We were given swarka by a street vendor. Then we were accosted by some Crestek males. They insulted Cat, and I answered their challenge."

"Cresteks harassed you and the female?" Karv's own face was stormy. "This is unacceptable. There is a peace between our peoples, and any Crestek knows better than to break the peace."

"I easily defeated the male who challenged me," Dev said, "but when I looked for Cat after the battle, she was gone."

"You do not think—?" Trek asked.

"That she left of her own free will?" Dev answered the unspoken question. "That she left us? No. She would not have done that. She was taken."

Trek sensed Karv stiffen.

"If this is true, then the Cresteks responsible will answer for this," he said, snatching his cloak from where it had been draped over a nearby console.

"I am grateful for your words, Karv." Dev's jaw was tight. "But we do not trust Crestek justice."

"Then let me prove that there are some Cresteks who believe in peace and a reunified people," Karv pulled up his sleeve to expose his markings.

"He was with the Crestek resistance," Trek told his brother.

Dev gave a single nod. "We will not hold the actions of a few again the honor of many. Your assistance is welcome."

Karv pulled on his cloak and headed for the door, talking as he walked. "Just like there was a Crestek resistance when we were enemies, there is an underground, separatist movement that believes the peace never should have happened, and that our people should remain at odds. They despise Dothveks."

"You think these separatists could be behind our mate's disappearance?" Trek pumped his arms as he and Dev jogged with Karv down the ramp that curved around the inside of the tall building.

"I would not be surprised. I can imagine no one else who would have the audacity to carry out the abduction of a female in broad daylight. There are enough separatists that they could have pulled this off and be hiding her in the city."

"So, they would not have taken her from the city?" Dev asked.

Karv lifted his chin and made a clicking sound with his tongue. "They would never venture beyond the city walls. They believe the sands are for barbarians." He cut a quick glance at the Dothveks. "Not that I believe that. I believe that we all came from the sands, where the goddess energy still powers the planet."

"You do not offend," Dev said. "The sands are our home. We are not ashamed of that." He eyed the Crestek. "You sound more like one of us than like your own kind."

Krav's mouth twitched into a brief smile. "Thank you. That is the greatest compliment you could pay me."

When they reached the bottom of the building, Krav paused at the door. "I do not know how we will find her, but we will go door to door if we need to."

Trek held up a fist. "We do not need to do that."

Dev locked eyes with his younger brother. "No, we do not." He released a breath. "I can sense her now too. She is not far from us."

Karv swiveled his head from one to the other. "You can sense her thoughts? I thought Dothveks could only sense the thoughts of other Dothveks."

"We can also sense our mind mates," Dev said, curling his hands into fists. "And right now, our mate is being held against her will. I feel her fear and her anger."

Then he took off running, with Trek and Karv close at his heels.

CHAPTER
TWENTY-THREE

Dev sensed Cat's anger and her fear, the messy mix of emotions driving him to rush through the Crestek city. He tore through the market square, dodging vendors and avoiding their displays with his brother, and the Crestek named Karv, behind him. As they left the crowded, open area and he darted down a narrow street with buildings looming high on either side, the tangle of thoughts quieted, and he was able to isolate Cat's voice from the others.

She was nearby, and she was being held against her will, but where?

Dev had never used his empathic abilities to locate someone, and he wasn't sure his skills could be used like that. Still, he had to try. Sensing his mate's fear was driving him mad.

He stopped at the intersection of several alleys and rested his hands on his knees as he let his head droop between his shoulders. "I don't know where she is."

Krav ran a hand through his short, dark hair as he swiveled his head to take in their surroundings. "You can hear her thoughts, though?"

"Faintly," Trek said, shrugging one shoulder when the Crestek looked at him in mild surprise. "We both share a mind bond with her."

"She's here," Dev told his brother. "She's close, but I don't know exactly where."

Krav peered at the dirty paving stones lining the alleys, and the dark doorways inset in the buildings. There were no colorful swaths of fabric draped over these narrow passageways, and even the suns didn't illuminate the shadowy corners. "If the separatists did take her, this would be the area they'd use to hold her."

"Why do you say that?" Trek asked.

Krav inclined his head. "No one asks questions in an area like this. If there are those who want to avoid the law, they'd be wise to hide out here."

Dev's lip twitched in distaste that the Crestek city harbored those who would willfully go against the interest of the clan. The Dothveks were raised to believe they were integrally connected to every member of their clan. A violation against one—or themself—was an injury to all.

Trek locked eyes with Dev. "Maybe you know more about where our mate is than you think, brother."

Dev closed his eyes and focused all his awareness on Cat. He reached out his own mind, sending her name into the ether and summoning her with everything he had. Even Trek's mind disappeared from his, as he blocked out every voice but hers. Finally, he sensed a pulse of recognition, and his own name echoed back to him.

Dev. Is that you?

He sucked in a breath, startled by how clear he could hear her in his mind. *It's me. Where are you?*

There was a long silence, and he feared he'd lost the connection. *I don't know. Someplace dark and damp.*

His heart sank. That could be anywhere. He shielded his disappointment from her, though. *Don't worry. We're coming for you.*

Hurry.

The tremor of fear in her request was a blade to his gut, and he gasped from the physical ache of it.

"Dev?"

Trek's voice pulled him back, and he opened his eyes.

"She's safe, but frightened."

Trek growled, pressing his angled brows together until they nearly met. "Where?"

"She doesn't know. Only that it is dark and damp."

"Damp?" Karv straightened. "That must mean she is being held underground, and in an area with bad drainage—like this one."

"That doesn't get us any closer to finding her." Dev scanned the tall buildings that extended endlessly in all directions.

Trek whipped the curved blade from his waist. "Then we go building to building and search."

Dev understood his brother's need to do something, but he also understood the look of horror that crossed Karv's face. Two Dothveks bursting into Crestek homes might not go over well, and it also might tip off those who were holding Cat. Word would spread before they might reach her, giving the abductors time to move her to another hiding place. He put a hand on his brother's arm. "We need to retain the upper hand and be stealthy. Even if we wish to tear the city apart to find her."

Trek heaved in a breath, his menacing expression relaxing after a tense moment. "Then what do you suggest?"

"If she was taken against her will, someone must have seen something," Karv said.

"The market square was crowded, and all eyes were on the fight," Dev said through gritted teeth, hating that he'd been so easily tricked into the battle that had provided the perfect distraction for Cat to be abducted.

"I do not think we ask the Cresteks in the market." Karv jerked his head up and clicked his tongue. "We need to find someone from the streets who sees everything."

Dev and Trek exchanged a look. Someone from the streets? They were unaware of his meaning. They'd grown up in an oasis tent village on the sands. There were no streets and no secrets. When only tent fabric separated you from your neighbor, and thoughts were passed from mind to mind as easily as by mouth, there was little you could keep to yourself.

Karv squinted down one alley and then another, his gaze finally alighting on a small figure flattened into a recessed doorway. He raced down the passageway and grabbed the child by the arm before he could flee.

"Whattcha doing?" the boy cried as he struggled to get away.

Dev and Trek caught up to Karv, startled that he held a boy who barely reached their waists. The Crestek boy stopped wiggling when he saw Dev and Trek, his jaw falling open and his eyes bugging out. Then his lower lip trembled.

"We only want to ask you some questions," Krav said.

Tears pooled in the boy's eyes. "You aren't going to let them eat me?"

Dev and Trek jerked back when they realized that the boy meant them. He was afraid that the Dothveks were going to devour him.

"We do not eat children," Dev said, "no matter what you might have heard about us."

The boy sniffled and wiped his nose with the back on his free hand, casting suspicious looks at the twins. "Promise?"

Karv gave his scruff a small shake. "If you tell us the truth."

The boy bobbed his head up and down. "What do you want to know?"

"Did you see a female who doesn't look like us?" Karv asked. "A human woman?"

"She would have been with some Cresteks," Dev added.

Recognition crossed the boy's dirty face. "Dressed like a boy with long hair and no cloak?"

Hope surged within Dev. "That's her. Did you see where she went?"

The boy nodded. "Two fellas were carrying her. Looked like she was sleeping." He scowled. "One of them kicked me and told me to beat it and stop staring."

Dev tempered his voice. "They don't sound nice."

Trek knelt to the boy's level. "I'll bet a smart boy like you noticed where they took her."

The boy gave him a half grin. "Sure did." He jerked a thumb behind him. "Next street over. The door with the handle that's crooked."

Krav handed the boy a dull, silver coin while Trek patted his shoulder. Dev didn't wait. He took off to find the door with the crooked handle, his heart thundering and anticipation making it hard for him to breathe.

CHAPTER
TWENTY-FOUR

Cat breathed in the dank air, tugging at the ropes binding her wrists. Her eyes had fully adjusted to the faint light, but she shivered from the cold and wished she was wearing her old clothes. She cut her gaze to the silky fabric that draped from the skinny straps on her shoulders and barely covered her cleavage. Did Crestek women really wear such flimsy outfits? The fabric was so sheer she suspected she'd be able to see through it in the light, which explained why they wore cloaks. Surely the males didn't wear such diaphanous garments.

This thought made a nervous giggle bubble up in her throat. Even though she was shivering and scared, she couldn't help laughing at the thought of the Cresteks in see-through pants. No Dothvek would wear something so impractical. Their leather pants were designed for the harsh environment of the desert and for moving quickly.

Thinking of the Dothveks—and of Dev and Trek—made an ache throb in her chest. She'd been able to sense Dev, and she knew he was close and that they were searching for her, but she couldn't tell him where she was. Her insistence on leaving the planet seemed so petty now. All she wanted was to be free and to see the twins again.

"Something funny?"

The raspy voice from the doorway made her jump. She hadn't noticed the crack in the door or the fact that her laughter had lingered. Cat pressed her lips together. The less she said, the better.

The Crestek who stepped into the room and pulled the door closed behind him wasn't the one who'd been in earlier. It was hard to make out features in the shadowy light, but she thought he was one of the goons who'd been behind the Crestek who'd challenged Dev. Which meant that he was probably one of the ones who jabbed her in the ass and dragged her off during the fight. More of a reason to say nothing to him.

He walked closer, bending down, and eyeing her openly. "Not in the mood to talk?"

Cat could see that he'd pushed back his hood, exposing his short hair and pointed ears. His eyebrows were dark slashes over his amber eyes. It was unnerving how much the Cresteks and Dothveks resembled each other, and she had to remind herself that they'd once been one people before becoming mortal enemies. How could the Cresteks see so much difference with the Dothveks when she saw so much alike?

When she didn't answer him, the Crestek smiled and put a hand on her knee. "You came to our city with two Dothveks. You must be something to satisfy two of those barbarians."

Cat clenched her jaw to keep from flinching as the alien moved his hand up her leg, taking the sheer fabric with it and exposing her bare skin. She would not give him the satisfaction of seeing her fear, so she held his gaze in challenge. "If I were you, I wouldn't touch a Dothvek's mate, and I really wouldn't want to touch the mate of *two* Dothvek warriors."

"Mate?" The Crestek choked out a laugh. "You think you're their mate?" He shook his head as if he pitied her. "Those barbarians might enjoy passing you around, but they aren't civilized enough to take wives like we do."

"I thought your women took multiple lovers." Cat couldn't resist snapping back at the alien's backward assumption. From what she'd seen, the Dothveks weren't the uncivilized ones. They weren't the ones taking women and holding them against their will. They didn't need to.

The Crestek let out a deep, menacing sound and squeezed her leg hard. Cat bit her lip to keep from crying out.

"Maybe we'll show you what it's like to take multiple Crestek lovers. Then you can decide if you like our way or theirs." He pushed her skirts all the way up and wrenched her knees apart as she fought to keep them closed.

Fear clawed at her throat, but then she was overcome with an even stronger sensation—rage. And it wasn't hers.

There was a loud crash from outside the room, followed by heavy thuds and muffled screams. The Crestek jumped back and spun around, but had barely reached the door when it flew open and sent him stumbling to the floor.

Dev and Trek rushed inside with blades drawn, their faces fierce as they looked to her and then to the Crestek on the floor. Dev reached down and lifted the alien by his neck, turning and throwing him forcefully from the room where he crashed loudly into something.

Trek hurried to her, pulling down her skirt and moving his hands over her. "Did they hurt you?"

Dev loomed behind him, breathing heavily. "Did they touch you?"

Cat let out a shaky breath as Trek untied her hands. "No, I'm fine."

"You are wearing Crestek clothes," Dev growled, frowning

at the sheer fabric that barely covered her, and then scowling at the motionless Crestek on the floor, as if he wished he could knock him out again.

When her hands were free, she leapt up and threw herself into Dev's arms. He staggered back before wrapping his strong arms around her and lifting her feet from the floor.

"You found me," she whispered into his neck as he held her. "You came for me."

"I will always come for you," he husked, burying his face in her hair. "We will always come for you."

Cat pulled back, smiling through blurry eyes, and turned to throw herself at Trek, who wrapped her in just as tight an embrace. "I hoped you would know that I didn't run off."

"We didn't think you'd run off," Trek reassured her. "Not when we were so close to getting you back to your ship."

Cat hesitated. Did she even care about her ship anymore? Was she willing to give up her life and her future to stay with two alien barbarians she barely knew?

As she opened her mouth to tell them she'd changed her mind about leaving, a Crestek ran into the room. This wasn't one of the ones who'd been holding her, and he wasn't wearing a cloak. Still, she huddled closer to Trek.

"This is Karv," he said, nodding to the Crestek. "He helped us find you."

Karv gave her an oddly formal bow before looking at Trek and then Dev. "I've tied up the criminals so they can be taken before the Crestek tribunal, but first you should come outside."

When no one moved, Karv beckoned with one arm. "A ship has just appeared over the city. Your kinsmen answered your hail."

CHAPTER
TWENTY-FIVE

Trek walked quickly from the building, keeping one arm firmly around Cat. He was so relieved to have found her unharmed, he wasn't willing to let her go for even a moment.

"This way." Karv jogged ahead as he led them back through the labyrinth of alleys and narrow passageways of the city. The dingy shadows gave way to wider streets and soon they were surrounded by chattering Cresteks all peering up at the sky from where the large bounty hunter ship descended.

Trek's heart lurched both with excitement and trepidation. He was glad that his kinsmen had responded so quickly to his hail, but he wasn't ready to let the female go. They'd just found her again. Was she truly going to go back to her ship after this?

His own emotions were in turmoil, and he could sense a similar restless unease within his brother. Neither of them would ever stoop to the level of the Cresteks and force their will on a female, but could they let her go? Trek had never believed that he and his brother would find a single mate they could share, much less one who shared a mind bond with each of them. How could they give her up?

Trek glanced over at Dev as they walked three across through the open gates of the city, at the same time as the ship touched down. The hot exhaust made dirt swirl into the air, and the noise of the engines was deafening as the huge ship powered down and the ramp began to lower.

He slipped his hand from Cat's waist and clasped her hand, noticing that his brother held her other hand. She peered up at him with a nervous smile, giving his hand a squeeze.

Trek tore his gaze from her. How could he say anything? She was clearly thrilled to be getting off his planet. All she'd wanted since she'd crashed in the sands was to return to her life and her ship. She wasn't cut out for a life as a Dothvek, even if she did have feelings for them. He steeled himself for what he needed to do as the metal ramped hit the ground and rattled from the impact.

The first Dothvek to clomp down the ramp was Vrax, and Trek's shoulder relaxed instantly. The warrior was younger than some of the others who'd taken bounty hunter mates, and he and Dev had fought in many battles by Vrax's side.

When Vrax spotted him, he beamed and ran the last few steps down the ramp. "When I saw that we had a hail from the twins, I wondered…" His words drifted off as his gaze drifted to the human standing between Trek and Dev. "Ah, now I understand."

Dev stepped forward and pulled Vrax into a back-thumping hug. "Do you?"

"This is Catarina," Trek said when Vrax and Dev separated. "She was a crew member aboard a space cruiser who was forced to abandon ship and landed here."

"You rescued her from the sands?"

Trek looked around Vrax to see K'alvek striding down the

ramp.

"Just as you found and saved your mate," Dev said, reminding the Dothvek of how he'd met the captain of the bounty hunter ship.

K'alvek grunted and nodded at Cat. "I hope my Dothvek brothers have treated you well."

Cat flushed and stammered, clearly overwhelmed by all the bare-chested Dothveks emerging from the ship, their chests and arms carrying various tribal markings. Despite living on a spaceship, the Dothveks still dressed as they did on the sands and looked like they were ready to spring into a battle.

"We know of a space cruiser from Earth that was forced to land on Carnack Prime for repairs," K'alvek said, crossing his arms over a broad chest that was adorned with black slashes.

"That's my ship," Cat said, bouncing on her toes. "Do you know if the crew is safe? Did everyone who abandoned ship return safely?"

K'alvek rocked back on his heels. "I do not know all the details, but I am aware of the crew being reassembled." He eyed her with curiosity, clearly perplexed why a human was dressed like a Crestek female. "You might be the crew member who ended up farthest from the ship."

"I had some difficulty with my pod," Cat said, her gaze dropping.

"But my kinsmen saved you."

Cat looked from Trek to Dev. "They did. Not only did they save me from being sucked under the sand with my pod, but they also saved me from a swarm of flying bugs and from some creepy Cresteks."

K'alvek's eyes widened, and his gaze slid to Dev and Trek and then to the Crestek Karv. "There is trouble with the peace?"

Karv stepped forward. "There are a few Crestek separatists,

but nothing that threatens the truce."

"Karv helped us send the transmission and find Cat," Trek said. "He also used to be a part of the Crestek resistance."

"Karv!"

All eyes went to the alien hurrying down the ramp. He was dressed like the other Dothveks, but his dark hair was short, and the markings on his chest were more ornate.

"T'Kar!" Karv rushed forward and clasped his arm. "It is good to see you again."

T'Kar pivoted to the other Dothveks. "Karv and I worked together in the Crestek resistance. He wished to be a Dothvek as much as I did."

Karv admired T'Kar's appearance, and the curved blade hooked to his waist. "You got what we both wanted."

"He earned it," Vrax said. "Now he's as much a Dothvek as any of us."

T'Kar squared his shoulders before tilting his head at his old friend. "You sent the transmission, Karv?"

"Apologies for not explaining everything in the hail," Karv said, "but Trek said he'd tell all when you arrived."

All eyes were on Trek, who flicked a gaze to his brother. "The human needs to be returned to her ship."

K'alvek appraised the twin warriors and the female standing between them. "We can return her to her ship. Carnack Prime is not far from our next mission." He let his pointed gaze linger on both warriors for a beat. "Is that all you need from us?"

Cat stepped forward shaking her head. "No."

"No, that's not all?" K'alvek asked. "How else can we assist you?"

Cat lifted her chin before spinning to face Dev and Trek with a fierce expression. "No, I don't want to go back to my ship."

CHAPTER
TWENTY-SIX

Dev stared at Cat, his heart filling with joy even as gut twisted. He forced the words from his mouth as if they were poison. "You should return to your ship. It's the future you want, and you would not be happy on our planet." He flicked a quick glance at his brother. "We do not want to be the reason for your unhappiness."

She put her hands on her hips. "Who says I would be unhappy?"

Dev was aware that the Dothveks from the bounty hunting ship were observing this conversation with interest, and part of him wished they were not standing at the bottom of the ship's ramp. "You have no desire to live in a tent on the sands, but that is our home."

She opened her mouth and then closed it, whatever argument she'd intended to make dying on her lips.

"You wish for a life free from struggle," he continued. "We can't offer you that."

"Brother," Trek said urgently, his voice low.

Dev shot him a look. "You wish to be the reason she sacrifices her dreams?"

Trek's shoulders sagged, and he pressed his lips together. Dev could sense his brother's dismay but also his realization that he was right. They couldn't keep Cat on their planet just because they were able to form a mind bond. She wasn't a Dothvek, and she wasn't used to their ways, or their world. Dev refused to talk her into staying and then being the reason she was miserable.

"Who says I would be miserable?" she snapped. "I never said that or thought it, so you might want to check out your mind-reading powers because I think you're glitching."

K'alvek and Vrax both went wide-eyed at this, but it was Trek who held up his hands.

"Dev doesn't mean to put words into your mouth, but can you truly tell us that you would give up life on your cruiser to stay on our planet? You were not fond of the *hashara*, and that is only one of the surprises of the sands."

"So, either I leave you both forever, or I have to stay here and live in a tent in the desert?" Cat's voice cracked as she swung her head from one brother to the other.

"There is another option."

Dev jerked his attention to the top of the ramp, frowning as Tommel strode down. His long hair was shot through with silver, and gray grizzled the stubble on his cheeks. His cheek was etched with intricate swirls that stretched across his shoulders.

Dev sensed his brother tense beside him. They had a bumpy past with the elder Dothvek, and Tommel had been the one to reject their request to join the bounty hunting crew not long ago. It was no secret that Tommel thought the twins to be impulsive and young, which was true when compared to his experience and cautious nature. Dev fought the urge to scowl when Tommel faced him.

"You think my decision before was unfair," the older Dothvek said as he crossed his arms over his chest.

It wasn't a question, so neither twin responded.

"I told you that unmated Dothveks would upset the balance of our bounty hunting crew," he continued. "I stand by that statement." His gaze slid to Cat. "But things appear to have changed."

Dev studied the Dothvek's solemn expression as the words sank in, but Trek was the first to speak.

"Do you mean you would consider allowing all three of us to join your crew?"

Tommel glanced at K'alvek, Vrax, and T'Kar. Although the Dothveks gave him the briefest of glances in return, it was enough. "We would."

K'alvek locked his gaze on Cat. "Then it is true you have bonded with both twins? You are mind mates with Dev and Trek?"

Cat gave the twins shy smiles before nodding. "It's true. I don't know how, but I can hear what both are feeling and thinking."

Tommel's slanted eyebrows rose. "Twin mind mating with a human female?"

Dev gave him a challenging look. "You don't believe us?"

"Twin mind mating is rare," Tommel said. "I believed the stories to be myth, but it is even more unbelievable that it would occur with a human."

Cat took both Dev's and Trek's hands. "Well, believe it, buddy."

Dev grinned at Tommel's startled expression. The elder had most certainly never been called *buddy* before.

Dev stepped closer to Cat but kept his gaze on Tommel.

"You must sense the truth of our claim. Otherwise, you wouldn't have suggested we join your crew."

Tommel inclined his head. "I wanted to hear it from the female. I also wanted to ascertain that you two had not sweet-talked her into something she didn't wish."

Trek laughed. "You have great regard for our charm."

"Perhaps." Tommel cocked his head. "I have seen it in action more than I care to admit."

Dev shifted from one foot to the other, the sand warm on his feet. He and Trek had befriended Tommel's mate before he had secured her, and they'd always regretted their brash and aggressive behavior toward the older Dothvek.

Dev squeezed Cat's hand, the softness of her skin sending a pulse of warmth through him. "We are not the same Dothveks we were."

Tommel's gaze swept across the threesome. Finally, he gave a single, sharp nod. "I can see that. The human has cooled the fires that stoked hot within you. You will make fine additions to our team."

Then Tommel turned and took long steps back up the ramp and disappeared into the ship.

Cat swung her head from Dev to Trek. "Does that mean we get to stay together?"

"As long as you don't mind joining our crew and being bounty hunters," Vrax said with a wink. "But don't worry, it's not a ship filled with Dothveks. There are plenty of human women on board."

"Really?" Cat's face brightened.

"Our captain is a female," K'alvek said, "and my mate."

"Fair warning," Vrax said from the side of his mouth. "There are also some babies on board, and they're not exactly quiet."

K'alvek frowned at Vrax, who held up his palms.

"I don't mind babies," Cat said, eagerly eyeing the ship before she bit her lower lip. "I don't suppose there's any way I could get a message to my friend on the cruiser to tell her I won't be returning."

"I can take care of that for you." T'Kar waved a hand as he started back up the ramp. "If you're ready to go."

"Are we?" Dev asked, holding Cat's eyes and ensuring she understood what she was agreeing to. As much as he loved his planet, he would eagerly make his life in space if he could make it with her. *Are you ready to spend the rest of your life as our mates?*

She beamed at him, and then Trek, squeezing both of their hands. "I'm more than ready."

CHAPTER
TWENTY-SEVEN

Cat followed Dev, as he followed the Dothvek called Vrax, as they wound through the ship.

"This is a Zevrian mercenary ship," Vrax said, as if that was explanation enough for the smooth, black walls and sleek interior. Beneath their feet, the engine hummed as they flew from the sand planet.

"What's a Zevrian?" She didn't know much about different alien species, but she was sure she'd never heard of the Zevrians.

"A species of serious badasses." Vrax glanced back at her. "Violent, short-tempered, skilled at killing."

Cat shuddered. "How is it you have their ship?" The question she didn't ask was if there were violent Zevrians looking for their ship.

Vrax grinned at her. "My mate is Zevrian. You'll meet her. She's the one who commandeered the ship, but now it flies as a joint human-Dothvek vessel. The Zevrians have no claim to it."

"How reassuring," Cat mumbled to herself as they

continued down the corridor, and she heard Trek chuckle behind her.

The interior of the ship was blessedly cooler than the hot, dusty surface of the sand planet, and the air carried the faint scent of fuel. Cat rubbed her arms briskly as she adjusted to the recirculated, cooled air piping from the ceiling vents. From behind her, Trek's large hands covered hers and the heat from his skin sent warmth through her.

Vrax paused in front of a handleless door that was as black as the glossy walls. "This will be your quarters for now." His gaze darted to Dev and then Trek. "Two smaller quarters connected by a bathing chamber. We can try to configure a larger, single—"

"It will be fine," Dev said before the Dothvek could finish.

Vrax's lips quirked. "I thought it would be." He touched his palm to a panel beside the door and it slid open silently. "Take your time settling in. We eat together in the ship's mess after third watch." He met both Dothveks' eyes for a beat. "We'll assign your ship duties tomorrow."

"I hope I get ship duties, too," Cat said. "I was a steward on a star cruiser." She didn't add that she stunk at the job. That was mostly because she was forced to deal with high-maintenance people. She doubted this ship had prima donnas like that.

Vrax grinned at her. "There are always things to be done on a ship. I'm sure the captain will put you to work."

Cat felt a strange sense of satisfaction as Vrax walked away, and Dev swept an arm wide to usher her into their quarters. She didn't feel overwhelmed like she had when she'd boarded the star cruiser, and she didn't feel embarrassed that she was sharing quarters with two Dothveks. So far, the bounty hunters had taken her arrangement with Dev and Trek in stride, accepting the mind bond the three of them shared without further question.

She stepped into the first of the two rooms and was glad there were two of them. The quarters were just what she'd expect from an alien mercenary ship—simple and utilitarian. The walls were as black as the ones in the corridor and arched up at the ceiling. There was a bed big enough for two fitted snugly with a dark gray blanket and topped with a pair of pillows. The nightstand was small and circular, with an attached, goose-necked light, and a black desktop jutted from the wall with a stool for it bolted to the floor.

Cat peeked into the open doorway into the bathroom, not surprised to see that it was all glossy, black tile, with another door opening into an identical bedroom. The towels hanging on the racks were the color of iron, and a spicy, male scent hung in the air.

She pivoted to face the twins. "So, how does this work? I get one room and you two share the other?" Their faces registered shock before she let a giggle escape. "I'm kidding, but you should see your faces."

Dev growled. "I will share you with my brother, but I will not share a bed with him alone."

"Nor will I," Trek said. "We have shared a tent, but we have always had separate furs."

"You also had separate women," Cat reminded them.

"This is different." Trek closed the distance between them and rested a hand on her hip as he faced her. "Sharing you does not feel like sharing."

Dev stepped closer and put a hand on her other hip, his body brushing the back of hers. "It feels like completion."

Her heart pounded as the two huge aliens pinned her from both sides, and she cleared her throat. "I don't know about you two, but I need a shower."

Trek ran his hands up her sides, taking the gossamer layers of the Crestek dress with them and pulling it over her head.

Cat stood in her panties, her jaw dangling. "What are you doing?"

"You said you wished to shower." Dev swiftly unhooked her bra from behind, and Trek pulled it down her arms, the twins working perfectly in sync. Then Trek cupped her breasts while his brother slid her panties down the length of her legs.

Her breath was ragged as Trek thumbed her nipples, but she managed to grab his pants and yank them down. When his angled brows peaked, she shrugged. "Turnabout is fair play." Then she turned and did the same to Dev's pants until both pairs were pooled around their ankles.

Trek half growled, half laughed as he tugged her backward toward the bathroom, and Dev followed, his eyes molten as they raked up and down her body. Trek flicked on the water, pulling Cat under the water flowing from multiple holes in the ceiling before it warmed up. She gasped at the cold water, her heart lurching and her skin pebbling as she attempted to back away.

"I will warm you," Dev husked, as he sandwiched her body from behind, the water rushing over all three of them as it slowly heated. He circled his arms around her back and palmed her breasts, as Trek's chest brushed her tight nipples.

Cat moaned, the heat of the Dothveks' bodies making her forget the tepid water as they ran their hands over her skin. She tipped her head back and let the water flow over her hair and wash away the dirt and grime of the past few days. The feel of the water and the two males one either side of her made all the fear and worry that had consumed her for so long melt away.

The feel of Trek's lips on hers made her catch her breath,

his kiss starting soft and tender and then deepening. His tongue parted her lips as he delved into her mouth. Dev's hands never stopped caressing her breasts, but soon he was pivoting her, snatching her lips from his brother, and claiming them for himself. She barely had a moment to breathe before he was kissing her, his lips even more forceful as he tangled his tongue with hers.

She moaned into his mouth as she submitted to him—to both of them. She was safe now. Dev and Trek would never let anything bad happen to her again. She was theirs, and they were hers. She released a groan. If being their mate and being possessed by them meant feeling so secure and safe and happy, then she never wanted to be apart from them again.

Pressing her palms against Trek's hard chest muscles, she started to lower herself.

"What are you—?"

She fisted his thick cock in one hand, and then took Dev's equally impressive cock in the other as Trek's words died out. The water continued to rush over them, but Cat barely noticed it, as she closed her lips over the broad crown of Trek's cock. It was wet and hot and deliciously slippery as she slid her mouth over it, bumping over each raised ring and sucking it as far down her throat as she could. Trek's moan filled the small bathroom and echoed off the tile.

Cat was filled with a thrill of empowerment as she pulled back and moved to Dev, taking him into her mouth and swirling her tongue around his head and each thick ring before she took all his rigid length down her throat. His dominant growl sent tingles down her spine as he fisted his hand in her hair.

Trek's hand joined his brother's to tangle in her hair, and they guided her head as she moved from one to the other, sucking them both until their desperate noises were so loud they reverberated through her bones. She loved that she was the one provoking such animalistic sounds, and she moaned her own pleasure around their cocks.

Before she could finish either of them, Dev grabbed her elbows and lifted her up, spinning her around and bending her over so she had to brace her hands against the slick, tile wall. The water was now hot and pounded on her back, as he and Dev positioned themselves behind her.

Dragging the head of his cock through her slickness, he notched himself at her opening before reaching around and finding her clit with his finger. He circled it as he slowly pushed into her, each one of his raised rings stretching her and making her bite down on her bottom lip.

When Cat twisted her head to look at him, Dev's gold skin glistened, and his chest muscles were taut as he looked down at where he was entering her. Trek stood next to him, his gaze scouring her body hungrily as he watched his brother fill her.

"You take my brother so well," he said over the sound of the water.

"Just like I'm going to take you," she told him, which made Trek growl.

Dev glanced at his brother. *Do you like to watch her stretched around my cock?*

Trek's eyes were dark with desire. *She's so tight.*

But she takes us so well.

Trek fisted his own cock as he watched Dev stroke in and out. Cat dropped her head between her shoulders, Dev's steady circling of her clit and their dirty thoughts about fucking her sending tremors through her body.

She moaned as her pussy clenched around Dev's cock, but as waves of pleasure rushed over her, she was aware of Dev pulling out and Trek thrusting himself inside her. The deep intrusion made her suck in breath as her release rippled through her, Trek holding himself deep.

He leaned over her, his lips buzzing her ear. "I wanted to feel you come on my cock."

Do you like coming on both of our cocks? Dev asked.

Cat hum-sighed her answer as her body continued to vibrate with pleasure, the idea that she'd come while both had been inside her arrowing another pulse of desire through her. She already felt drugged with endorphins, even though the twin Dothveks weren't done with her.

She's even tighter now, brother, Trek told Dev, and he weaved his fingers into her wet hair and pulled her head back so he could crush his lips to hers. His tongue stroked hers with the same punishing pace as his cock thrust inside her. *And she tastes so good.*

The ship seemed to shift as Trek drove into her again and again, his lips as insistent as his cock as it plundered her. Then his pace quickened, and he threw back his head and roared, emptying into her.

Then he pulled out, and Dev pulled her to standing and spun her around to face him. He hoisted her up, so her legs were around his waist, and he drove her down on his cock. Cat inhaled sharply, bracing her hands on his slippery shoulders as he held her ass and moved her up and down.

"My brother was right," he panted. "You're even tighter on my cock."

She's perfect. Trek circled his arms around her from behind and cupped her breasts, rolling her hard nipples between his fingers as Dev watched with unbridled hunger.

"We're both going to fill you." Dev pumped her faster on his cock. "Do you want that?"

She nodded desperately.

We're both going to fuck you like this every night, Dev's brow was furrowed intensely. *You like that, don't you? You like to take us together. One cock after the other.*

Flames licked Cat's skin as she rolled her head back and moaned in surrender.

Not just every night. Trek nuzzled her neck. *I want to wake up inside you.* He pinched her nipples. *With your lips wrapped around my brother's cock.*

Her body trembled as she gasped out, "maybe even together."

Both Dothveks stilled for a beat, then Dev locked his gaze on hers. "At the same time?"

"Are you sure you can take us both?" Trek murmured, his hot breath buzzing her ear from behind.

Her answer was to tip forward and tilt her ass up. Trek ran has hands down her body and squeezed her ass cheeks as she offered them to him, his own desperate moan escaping from his mouth.

"I want to," she whispered, her desire overtaking any fear or nervousness.

"You heard the female," Dev said, pinning his brother's gaze over her shoulder. "*Our* female."

Trek made a rough, guttural noise as he pressed the crown of his cock at her tight opening, then he slowly entered her while Dev held himself inside her without moving.

Cat sucked in a sharp breath, the stretch making her press her lips together to keep from screaming. It was strange that something should dance on the knife's edge of pleasure and pain, and she bit her bottom lip hard as she took each ridge of Trek's thick cock.

Both Dothveks moved gingerly. Dev stroked her hair while Trek ran his hands down the length of her back until he'd completely filled her. Then all three of them dragged in ragged breaths as she adjusted to the sensation of being filled by both of their cocks. It was so intense she couldn't speak, until the words burst from her.

"I need you both to fuck me."

Dev jerked at the command, but Trek grabbed a fistful of her hair and tangled his fingers in it, pulling her back as he started to stroke in and out.

Now you, brother. Trek's face was fierce as Cat glanced back at him, and she thrilled at the sight of his barely-controlled need.

Dev grunted as he clutched her hips and moved her up and down to match his brother's movements. His brow was furrowed and sweat trickled down the side of his face as he looked at Cat with near reverence. *You are more perfect than I could have imagined.*

She smiled as her eyelids fluttered. "I never thought I could find one guy as good as this, but two is even better."

She was made for us, brother. Trek leaned forward and kissed the back of her neck. *Being inside her with you is like being one with a goddess.*

Tremors shook Cat as a powerful release made her grasp Dev's shoulders and dig her nails in his flesh. At that moment, she felt every bit the goddess. *Their* goddess. She screamed as her body clenched around both cocks, the waves of pleasure crashing into her like a tsunami.

At this, Dev pistoned hard into her, driving her down and holding himself deep as he exploded inside her. Then Trek stroked into her once more before throwing back his head and roaring as he pulled out and pulsed hot on her back. As she gasped for breath, Trek laughed low and whispered into Cat's ear as his brother's cock was still hard inside her. "Is that how you like it, mate?"

All her nerve endings were on fire as tried to remember how to breathe. Even though her mind was a euphoric daze, she knew one thing. She did want everything both of them could give her. She wanted to take both twins just like this. Cat locked eyes with Dev and then hooked her arm around Trek's neck behind her. *I do.*

EPILOGUE

Maya stepped tentatively from the shuttlecraft and peered up at the towering stone walls surrounding the city. This was where the transmission had originated? Cat was somewhere inside this alien city?

She flipped her black curls off her shoulder and inhaled the hot air, already wishing that she was back on the climate-controlled ship. "This heat is going to fuck with my hair."

Not that she would be on the alien planet for long. She was there to get Cat and take her back to the repaired ship, so she'd have to suck up the heat and the sand. She groaned as her boot sank into the powdery gold granules. Too bad there wasn't a cool expanse of blue water attached to the sand.

"I'll find Cat and be right back," she called over her shoulder to the shuttle pilot.

"You want me to go with you?"

She eyed the open gates and remembered the transmission. "No. The aliens on the planet aren't supposed to be dangerous.

Besides, Cat sent a message about them saving her. I'll go in, grab her, and we'll head out."

"Suit yourself."

Maya rolled her eyes. The pilot who'd flown her wouldn't have been much help, anyway. He was one of the third stringers, and he seemed to prefer napping to anything else. She glanced back at the cockpit and could see that he already had his feet propped on the console, and his head was tipped back on the headrest.

She guessed she should be grateful that she was allowed to take a shuttle in the first place. The only reason the space cruiser captain allowed it was because they were still waiting for repairs to be finished before loading all the passengers and resuming their flight. She doubted he'd have humored her even to retrieve one of the upper deck stewards if they'd been ready to fly. The ship was already behind schedule, which meant the privileged passengers were annoyed, which meant the captain was taking the heat. The second they were ready to go, the cruiser would depart—missing steward back on board, or not.

"Let's do this," Maya said under her breath as she trudged forward.

The thick gates loomed as she entered the city, and her gaze went to the shimmering domes and brightly colored fabric crisscrossing overhead. Despite its ancient appearance, the Crestek city clearly had the technological capacity to send transmissions, which meant it couldn't be as backward as it seemed when they'd descended to the sand-covered planet.

She was aware that she was the only one not wearing a long robe and hood as she moved tentatively through a central square, gazes swiveling to her and hems flapping as natives turned to watch. Obviously, they didn't get many visitors.

Maya searched the crowd for a glimpse of Cat. The woman

had to be there somewhere. She had sent a transmission that she was on the planet, although it had been vague. Maya assumed she'd be in the only city they'd detected on their scans of the planet. If she was somewhere else, the search was going to take a lot longer than she'd planned.

"You're human."

Maya spun at the statement, tipping her head up to meet the eyes of the alien who stood smiling down at her. The hood of his robe was pushed back, revealing pointed ears poking through short dark hair. Like all the natives she'd seen so far, his skin was a deep-gold hue.

"I am." She returned his smile. "You don't seem surprised to see a human here."

"You aren't the first human female I've encountered."

Her pulse quickened. "Do you know my friend Cat? Do you know where she is?"

"Yes, and yes." The alien bowed his head slightly. "I am Karv. I sent the transmission that probably brought you here."

Maya released a breath. "Whew. I was starting to wonder if I was in the right place."

"You are in the right place, but your friend is no longer in our city."

Maya face fell. "What? Where did she go?"

Karv tilted his head. "It is a long story, but I will explain everything while I take you to our communications hub where you can send a transmission to her new ship."

"New ship?" Maya rubbed her forehead, glancing behind her at the open gates then back to the friendly—and hot—alien. This guy seemed like her best bet to find out what happened to her friend, and she could still leave and get back to her shuttle before nightfall.

"Your friend Catarina had a bit of an adventure while she was on our planet, but I assure you she's safe." Karv took a few steps and then stopped and waited for her to follow him. "I should be able to connect you to her ship so you can talk to her."

Maybe it was the alien's smile, but she trusted him even though she'd just met him, and she was alone in an alien city. She was dying to find out what had happened to Cat, and this guy appeared to have the answers. She sighed and shrugged off her hesitation as she followed him. "Lead on."

On the edge of the city square, a Crestek in a long, silver robe observed Karv and Maya with his eyes narrowed. The new Crestek chancellor turned to one of his aides. "Who is the alien female?"

A pudgy Crestek peeked from under his purple hood. "A human, excellency. She arrived on a shuttle, which is outside the city gates."

"Just her?"

"The pilot remained in the vessel. I assume he awaits her return."

"And why is she here?"

"Her request to land mentioned locating her shipmate, the human who left with the Dothveks and the bounty hunters."

The chancellor flipped back his hood, revealing a youthful face and intense, amber eyes. "The one who was taken by the separatists?"

The aide's gaze lowered. "Yes."

"These humans are quite alluring, aren't they?" The chancellor's gaze tracked Maya walking next to Karv. "It's too bad all the ones who previously came to our planet were claimed by Dothveks." His lip curled, as his aide's head snapped up. "Maybe we can change that."

"Excellency?"

The chancellor's pupils darkened as he watched the human vanish into the crowd. "Take me to the separatists who're being held for their failed abduction attempt." He licked his lower lip and let out a low growl. "I have a task for them."

THANK YOU FOR READING PRIZE! If you'd like to read a steamy bonus epilogue with Cat and her two barbarians (and become one of my VIP Readers), click below:

https://BookHip.com/PHWGJXN

WANT MORE to find out what happens to Maya? Read SECRET, the next book in the series!

"Maya and Karv were so perfect for each other and their chemistry was fantastic. Their banters and teasings were so much fun to read... the passionate moments they shared were off-the-charts hot and I couldn't get enough!" - Amazon Reviewer

One-click SECRET!

∽

This book has been edited and proofed, but typos are like little gremlins that like to sneak in when we're not looking. If you spot a typo, please report it to: tana@tanastone.com

Also by Tana Stone

The Tribute Brides of the Drexian Warriors Series:

TAMED (also available in AUDIO)

SEIZED (also available in AUDIO)

EXPOSED (also available in AUDIO)

RANSOMED (also available in AUDIO)

FORBIDDEN (also available in AUDIO)

BOUND (also available in AUDIO)

JINGLED (A Holiday Novella) (also in AUDIO)

CRAVED (also available in AUDIO)

STOLEN (also available in AUDIO)

SCARRED (also available in AUDIO)

ALIEN & MONSTER ONE-SHOTS:

ROGUE (also available in AUDIO)

VIXIN: STRANDED WITH AN ALIEN

SLIPPERY WHEN YETI

CHRISTMAS WITH AN ALIEN

YOOL

Raider Warlords of the Vandar Series:

POSSESSED (also available in AUDIO)

PLUNDERED (also available in AUDIO)

PILLAGED (also available in AUDIO)

PURSUED (also available in AUDIO)

PUNISHED (also available on AUDIO)

PROVOKED (also available in AUDIO)

PRODIGAL (also available in AUDIO)

PRISONER

PROTECTOR

PRINCE

The Barbarians of the Sand Planet Series:

BOUNTY (also available in AUDIO)

CAPTIVE (also available in AUDIO)

TORMENT (also available on AUDIO)

TRIBUTE (also available as AUDIO)

SAVAGE (also available in AUDIO)

CLAIM (also available on AUDIO)

CHERISH: A Holiday Baby Short (also available on AUDIO)

PRIZE (also available on AUDIO)

SECRET

RESCUE (appearing first in PETS IN SPACE #8)

Inferno Force of the Drexian Warriors:

IGNITE (also available on AUDIO)

SCORCH (also available on AUDIO)

BURN (also available on AUDIO)

BLAZE (also available on AUDIO)

FLAME (also available on AUDIO)

COMBUST

THE SKY CLAN OF THE TAORI:

SUBMIT (also available in AUDIO)

STALK (also available on AUDIO)

SEDUCE (also available on AUDIO)

SUBDUE

STORM

All the TANA STONE books available as audiobooks!

INFERNO FORCE OF THE DREXIAN WARRIORS:

IGNITE on AUDIBLE

SCORCH on AUDIBLE

BURN on AUDIBLE

BLAZE on AUDIBLE

FLAME on AUDIBLE

RAIDER WARLORDS OF THE VANDAR:

POSSESSED on AUDIBLE

PLUNDERED on AUDIBLE

PILLAGED on AUDIBLE

PURSUED on AUDIBLE

PUNISHED on AUDIBLE

PROVOKED on AUDIBLE

BARBARIANS OF THE SAND PLANET

BOUNTY on AUDIBLE

CAPTIVE on AUDIBLE

TORMENT on AUDIBLE

TRIBUTE on AUDIBLE

SAVAGE on AUDIBLE

CLAIM on AUDIBLE

CHERISH on AUDIBLE

TRIBUTE BRIDES OF THE DREXIAN WARRIORS

TAMED on AUDIBLE

SEIZED on AUDIBLE

EXPOSED on AUDIBLE

RANSOMED on AUDIBLE

FORBIDDEN on AUDIBLE

BOUND on AUDIBLE

JINGLED on AUDIBLE

CRAVED on AUDIBLE

STOLEN on AUDIBLE

SCARRED on AUDIBLE

SKY CLAN OF THE TAORI

SUBMIT on AUDIBLE

STALK on AUDIBLE

SEDUCE on AUDIBLE

About the Author

Tana Stone is a bestselling sci-fi romance author who loves sexy aliens and independent heroines. Her favorite superhero is Thor (with Aquaman a close second because, well, Jason Momoa), her favorite dessert is key lime pie (okay, fine, *all* pie), and she loves Star Wars and Star Trek equally. She still laments the loss of *Firefly*.

She has one husband, two teenagers, two dogs, and three neurotic cats. She sometimes wishes she could teleport to a holographic space station like the one in her tribute brides series (or maybe vacation at the oasis with the sand planet barbarians). :-)

She loves hearing from readers! Email her any questions or comments at tana@tanastone.com.

Want to hang out with Tana in her private Facebook group? Join on all the fun at: https://www.facebook.com/groups/tanastonestributes/

Copyright © 2022 by Broadmoor Books

Cover Design by Croco Designs

Editing by Tanya Saari

All rights reserved.

No part of this book may be reproduced in any form or by any electronic or mechanical means, including information storage and retrieval systems, without written permission from the author, except for the use of brief quotations in a book review.

This is a work of fiction. Names, characters, places, and incidents are the products of the author's imagination or are used fictitiously and are not to be construed as real. Any resemblance to actual events, locales, organizations, or persons, living or dead, is entirely coincidental.

Made in United States
North Haven, CT
21 June 2025